"This is o

Nick placed his hands on his sons' shoulders. "We're renting now, but the owners are thinking about selling."

This was getting more unbelievable by the second.

"Mrs. Buser mentioned yesterday that we'd be neighbors. I guess it's true what they say about it being a small world." He scratched the side of his head and crinkled his brow.

Neighbors? What was that old saying Joy had heard? Good fences make good neighbors—or something like that. That was it—she'd build a fence as high as her homeowners' association would allow. She was president; she should know the restrictions. She'd have to check the covenants. Even still, building a wall around her property wouldn't keep Nick out of her heart. "But this is my neighborhood. I moved here after college."

"She lives right over there, Daddy," Tyler announced, pointing in the direction of Joy's one-story ranch home. "Isn't that cool? Maybe she'll invite us over for dinner sometime."

This definitely wasn't cool. Dinner? Absolutely not. How would she avoid Nick when he'd be just outside her door?

Weekdays, **Jill Weatherholt** works for the City of Charlotte. On the weekend, she writes contemporary stories about love, faith and forgiveness. Raised in the suburbs of Washington, DC, she now resides in North Carolina. She holds a degree in psychology from George Mason University and a paralegal studies certification from Duke University. She shares her life with her real-life hero and number one supporter. Jill loves connecting with readers at jillweatherholt.com.

Books by Jill Weatherholt

Love Inspired

A Mother
for His Twins

Jill Weatherholt

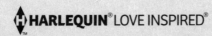
HARLEQUIN® LOVE INSPIRED®

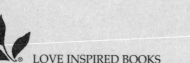

LOVE INSPIRED BOOKS

Recycling programs
for this product may
not exist in your area.

ISBN-13: 978-1-335-47941-9

A Mother for His Twins

Copyright © 2019 by Jill Weatherholt

All rights reserved. Except for use in any review, the reproduction
or utilization of this work in whole or in part in any form by any
electronic, mechanical or other means, now known or hereafter
invented, including xerography, photocopying and recording, or in
any information storage or retrieval system, is forbidden without
the written permission of the editorial office, Love Inspired Books,
195 Broadway, New York, NY 10007 U.S.A.

This is a work of fiction. Names, characters, places and incidents are
either the product of the author's imagination or are used fictitiously, and
any resemblance to actual persons, living or dead, business establishments,
events or locales is entirely coincidental.

This edition published by arrangement with Love Inspired Books.

® and TM are trademarks of Love Inspired Books, used under license.
Trademarks indicated with ® are registered in the United States Patent
and Trademark Office, the Canadian Intellectual Property Office and in
other countries.

www.Harlequin.com

Printed in U.S.A.

Therefore if any man be in Christ, he is a
new creature: old things are passed away;
behold, all things are become new.
                    —*2 Corinthians* 5:17

To my beautiful mother.

Your support, encouragement and constant love have sustained me throughout my life.

Chapter One

If the rancid coffee was an indication of the day ahead, perhaps Joy Kelliher should have stayed in bed. Settling into her favorite leather chair in the teachers' lounge at Whispering Slopes K-12, she leaned toward the frosty window, pushing her thick brunette hair away from her face. She treasured the early morning hours before the school bustled with children. It was the second week in January, and the Virginia mountain community, nestled in the Shenandoah Valley, had yet to experience their first major snowfall of the season. Smiling, Joy eyed a white-tailed deer as it meandered across the playground, leaving its footprints in the dusting of snow that had fallen overnight. Spooked, it raced off into the forest that lined the school grounds. Fear. She knew it well.

A knock at the open door jarred the first-grade teacher before her mind spiraled down that dark road.

"Joy, I'd like to introduce you to your two new students."

Mr. Jacobson stood in the doorway. A small, thick man with thinning gray hair, he'd taken over as principal after her father passed away when she was only two years old. With his retirement date nearing, her dream to work with and protect all of the children in the school, not just those in her classroom, could finally come true. She'd begun preparing for an interview the moment Mr. Jacobson had announced his retirement.

"This is Jordan and Tyler Capello," he said, guiding two brown-haired, rosy-cheeked boys into the room.

Capello. No, it can't be. Joy rubbed her eyes. The wood chair screeched as she pushed her slender frame from her seat. Was she seeing double?

The principal chuckled. "Yes, they're twins. Identical. You'll have your hands full." He turned toward the door. "I believe you know their father." He extended his right arm. "Nick, don't be shy. Come on in, son."

Heat prickled the back of her neck. She gripped the edge of the chair to steady herself. Nick Capello. This couldn't be happening. Not after fourteen years of silence—of heartache.

Her heart pummeled against her rib cage as he slowly approached her—all six feet five inches of him. No longer the boy she remembered. With his Italian good looks, he'd grown into a strikingly handsome man who could still make her knees wobble like a newborn colt's.

"Hello, Joy." He reached for one of her hands, which she kept fisted at the sides of her thighs.

She swallowed once and then again before risking another glance in his direction. The lump lodged in her throat didn't budge. "What…? Why…? What are you doing here?"

The once extended hand raked through his dark hair. His piercing blue eyes locked with hers. "This is my home. It's always been. My boys are going to experience the joys of growing up in a small town, just like I did. I want that sense of community for them."

His home? How could he call Whispering Slopes home? He and his family had moved in the dark of night, leaving a small town asking questions and her heart smashed in a million tiny pieces.

Her shoulders squared. "This isn't your home." Once it had been, but that was a lifetime ago.

One of the twins with a slightly larger frame stepped forward and flashed a smile that revealed two missing front teeth. "I'm Tyler, and this is my brother, Jordan. He might not talk much, but that doesn't mean he doesn't like you—he's just shy, that's all."

Her heart squeezed as she studied the boy with freckles that dotted his nose. He was the spitting image of his father at that age. She would know. She'd known Nick all of her life. They'd grown up together and had fallen in love. During their senior year of high school they'd made a plan. After graduation, they'd marry and have a house full of children. Joy had never been happier... and then it was all stripped away.

Nick placed his hands on Tyler's shoulders and eyed Joy. "I'm sorry if I've caught you off guard. Maybe I should have called first."

In order to maintain her professionalism, she drew in a slow and steady breath. She'd worked too hard to establish her reputation at this school. She forced a smile as she glanced at the twins. "Welcome to Whispering Slopes, boys."

Mr. Jacobson cleared his throat. "Nick, why don't we leave the boys here to get better acquainted with Miss Kelliher? We'll go down to the office and get them registered. Then we can get your paperwork taken care of so you can start subbing on Monday."

Joy's head spun toward the principal. "Excuse me?"

"Nick's going to take over Mrs. Murray's classroom while she's out on maternity leave." Mr. Jacobson smiled at Joy. "I can't tell you how thrilled I am to have former students teaching at the school. You two will be right across the hallway from each other."

Nick's gaze burned the side of her face. She couldn't look at him. Not now. The pain from the past bubbled to the surface like cooking oil poured into a pot of boiling water. No. She wouldn't cry in front of him. Too many tears had been shed over this man.

Nick knelt in front of his boys. "Are you two going to be okay?"

"Sure, Daddy," they replied in unison as their father stood.

Jordan didn't look as certain as his brother. Tyler had spoken the truth. He appeared to be more timid than his twin.

"Okay, then. I'll be back to pick you up at three o'clock. We'll go out for ice cream and you can tell me all about your first day."

She watched as the boys' eyes lit up, shaking off the memory of how Nick's eyes had done the same whenever she'd entered a room. They'd been so in love. She almost smiled at the memory.

"See you later, Daddy."

Nick turned to Joy. "Right across the hall, so I guess we'll be seeing a lot of each other." He flashed a crooked smile.

She remained silent. Fourteen years had passed and Nick had been silent, too. He'd never once called or even sent a letter to explain why one minute he'd been in her life and then he'd vanished. It took years for her to get past the pain. But really, had she ever stopped hurting? Did the constant yearning to feel his arms around her one more time ever really go away? Seeing Nick now, she realized the wounds remained fresh.

He dropped his gaze to the ground. With his shoulders slumped, he left the room.

Painful memories surged like a massive lightning bolt on a steamy August afternoon. *Lord, how can You let this happen? I can't teach these boys. Is this some sort of punishment? Didn't I suffer enough on that night fourteen years ago?*

She watched as the twins peered out the window toward the playground, chattering in whispered tones. *I can do this.* She exhaled. "So, would you like to go outside and play for a while?"

They both turned and eagerly nodded their heads.

"We've got half an hour before class starts." The sun had already begun to melt the dusting of snow. "Make sure you zip up your coats."

Outside on the playground, Joy used a paper towel to wipe off the bench closest to the swings and took a seat. Tyler took the towels she'd given them and cleared the teeter-totter before helping his brother climb aboard. She smiled. He definitely was his brother's protector.

Inhaling the brisk mountain air, she pulled her phone from the pocket of her jacket to call her twin sister, Faith. Having lost their parents at a young age, they leaned on each other in difficult times. Throughout their lives, Faith had served as Joy's lighthouse, guiding her through every storm, especially after that horrible night. Her twin was the only one who knew about the attack, but nothing more. Before that evening, Joy had always shared everything with Faith, but what happened weeks later was something she couldn't bear to tell anyone—not even her closest confidante. As she punched the number for the resort, she kept a close eye on the boys.

"Thank you for calling the Black Bear Resort. This is Faith."

What was formerly a small inn had grown into a larger resort. Her sister was living her dream, running the business along with a wonderful man, Joshua. They'd married last year and now they were expecting twins. Bella—Faith's daughter from her first husband, who'd died tragically fighting a fire—was thrilled to know two babies would soon join their family.

"Hey, can you talk?"

"What's up, sis?"

"Well, I'm sitting here on the playground watching my two newest students… Twins." Joy pressed her palm into the arm of the cedar bench. "They're Nick's kids." Saying it out loud made it more real.

"Oh, my. I always knew he'd come back, but I didn't expect him to return with children."

Joy hadn't anticipated either scenario. "Why did you think he'd return to Whispering Slopes?"

Faith laughed. "Because of you, of course."

"That's crazy. He's got children, so he must have a wife. Besides, he's come back to teach." The thought of working so closely with him seemed like a bad dream. "I can't believe this is happening. His presence makes everything feel like it just happened yesterday." Her words sparked a shiver.

"You need to talk with him and tell him what happened to you, Joy."

Her stomach rolled over at the thought. How could she ever talk to him about that night she'd been waiting for him at the pond? "I don't think I can. Besides, what's the point?"

"Talking about it might help with the healing process. It's been fourteen years… You've got to let it go."

Sprigs of partially frozen fescue flattened underneath her feet. "I don't think I can. I'm too ashamed. Besides, it won't change the past. Can we move on to another subject? I want to forget about Nick Capello."

"That's going to be a little hard given the fact that you'll be teaching his kids and working together."

"I'll just treat him like any other parent or coworker." Joy knew convincing herself of that would be easier said than done.

"But he's not."

The truth in Faith's words stung. "He's a stranger to me now." She spied the boys climbing off the teeter-totter. Once again, Tyler assisted Jordan. "I've got to go. Thanks for listening."

"Are you sure you're okay?"

"Yeah—I'll be fine." Joy ended the call just as the twins approached. The knot in her stomach squeezed a little tighter knowing she hadn't been truthful with her sister. From now until the end of the school year, she'd have a constant reminder of a love lost. But it wasn't fair to the boys for her to treat them differently. Despite the resemblance, somehow she'd have to forget their father was the love of her life. "It's a little cold. Are you ready to go inside?"

They exchanged a quick glance with one another. Tyler spoke first. "We'd rather stay out here with you."

She knew that look… Fear. "Don't you want to meet

your new classmates? I'm sure they'll be excited to welcome you."

Jordan kicked his tennis shoe into the wet ground. "They pwobably won't like us."

Joy noticed Jordan struggled with the letter *r*. She rested her hand on the boy's shoulder. "What makes you say that?"

Tyler hopped up on the bench next to her. "The kids at our old school didn't."

What was not to love about these enchanting children? "Could it have been your imagination?"

Jordan took his brother's lead and plopped on the other side of his teacher. "No, they didn't." He spoke softly.

Tyler glanced up toward the sky. "They said we were different because we looked alike."

Kids could be so cruel sometimes. "You know what I think?" Joy stood and then knelt in front of the bench. "I think maybe they were jealous because they knew you were guaranteed to always have a best friend."

Tyler's eyebrow arched exactly how his father's always had. "What do you mean?"

"When you're a twin, you've got a best friend for life. You know someone who always has your back. I'm a twin. Not identical like the two of you, but I know what I'm talking about."

Grins washed across their faces.

"If anyone ever teases you again you tell them you're so special, God had to make two of you."

In one swift movement, the twins wrapped their arms around her. She pulled back—frightened by the tug she felt on her heart. "So, you haven't told me anything about yourselves. Where did you live before you came to Whispering Slopes?"

"In Chicago." Jordan answered first.

"That's where our mommy was born." Tyler's smile faded.

"She died there, too," Jordan added.

Joy had wondered about their mother and why she hadn't come with Nick to registration. Now she knew. The tear that puddled in the corner of sweet little Jordan's eye caused her heart to squeeze. She knew the pain of losing a parent at a young age.

"We didn't really want to move, but Daddy wants to teach where he grew up," Tyler explained as he jumped off the bench at the sound of the school bell. "He's going to be the new principal, too." The child reached for her hand as they strolled toward the building.

What? That was impossible. The boys must have misunderstood. Nick couldn't be here for that job. The knot in her stomach squeezed a little tighter. She'd been studying hard to obtain her master's degree and had nearly completed the program. There was only one opening for a principal in Whispering Slopes—and it belonged to her.

"Here's the list of school supplies we need. Miss Kelliher said to go to Buser's General Store. They've got the best prices." Tyler pulled the crinkled piece of paper from his superhero backpack and handed it to his father.

Nick smiled at his son. He always liked to be in charge, while Jordan seemed to follow his brother's lead.

The twins' half-eaten ice cream sundaes were turning into milky soup. Since they'd arrived at One More Scoop, they'd chattered nonstop about their first day of school.

Seeing his boys so excited helped to ease some of the

painful memories and the guilt that haunted him. Nick smiled at the familiar chalkboard hanging on the wall behind the register. The menu listed all of the specialty flavors of ice cream. They still made Coke floats. Everything looked exactly how it had when he was a kid. It even smelled the same, like a sugary waffle cone on a boardwalk during the height of summer.

Jordan scooped a spoon of the melted dessert from his bowl and held it to his lips. "All of the kids wuh weally nice."

Nick laughed as the treat dribbled down his chin. It made him happy to know his son had had a good day. Jordan struggled at times in social situations due to his speech impairment. Nick yanked a napkin from the holder and passed it to his son. "Here, I think you need this."

"Yeah, and no one teased us about looking alike either," Tyler added.

Jordan wiped his mouth as the whirl of a blender charged from behind the counter. "Even if they had, Miss Kellihuh told us what to say. She's weally nice."

Nick's ears perked up at the mention of Joy's name. There was a part of him that had hoped he'd run into Joy, but when he'd made the decision to move home, he never imagined his first love would end up teaching his sons. "What did she tell you?"

"She said if someone teased us to tell them we were so special God made two of us," Tyler said, wearing a huge grin. "She's really cool."

He closed his eyes for a second and pictured Joy's face. Her response to the boys was exactly what he'd expect. It's what he'd loved most about her. She always knew what to say at the perfect time. "She's right, you know."

"She's a twin, too." Jordan picked up his bowl and started to drink the melted ice cream.

Nick reached for his arm. "Use your manners, son."

"Sowwy." He put the treat back onto the red-and-white-checkered tablecloth and fidgeted in his seat.

"Yeah, Daddy, Miss Kelliher has a twin sister." Tyler took a sip of his water. "But they're not identical like us."

Growing up, Nick remembered Joy wishing she and Faith were identical. Her twin was good in math while Joy struggled. She always thought it would be nice if Faith could take her place on the days they had a test. "Yes, I know."

The boys looked at each other with crinkled brows. "How?" they asked in unison.

Nick wasn't ready to tell the boys that, once upon a time, he and their teacher had had plans to marry. "Miss Kelliher and I grew up running around in our diapers together."

The twins covered their faces and giggled.

"That's funny," Jordan said. "I like huh."

"She's really pretty." Tyler spoke up. "Don't you think, Daddy?"

Nick hesitated.

"Yeah, Daddy, don't you think so?" Jordan asked.

Nick's heartbeat quickened. Their mother and Joy were both the most beautiful women he'd ever known. Different in their own ways, but the one common denominator was their loving and compassionate hearts. His stomach twisted at the thought of Michelle suffering in silence from complications of Crohn's disease. He should have noticed. Since she'd passed away a year ago last November, the guilt had gnawed away at him each day, but more so at night.

Nick shook off the negative thoughts. "Come on now and finish up your ice cream so we can get your supplies."

The boys exchanged a quick glance.

Nick watched Jordan as he pushed his bowl aside. He hoped bringing his boys back to Whispering Slopes wasn't creating more anxiety over their mother's death.

Thirty minutes later the bell on the door chimed as Nick and the boys entered Buser's General Store. Nick's heart warmed. Just like One More Scoop, it was as though time had stood still. The scent of cinnamon swirled in the air. He'd always loved the swizzle candy sticks sold in the giant jar. The sound system played a continuous playlist of songs from the 1950s. He smiled when he spotted a young boy and girl, probably in high school, sharing a cream soda at the counter. How many times had he and Joy sat in that same spot, excited about their future?

He turned when the door tinkled. The trip down memory lane came to a screeching halt.

"Miss Kelliher!" All smiles, Tyler and Jordan sprinted across the room.

Nick swallowed hard while he observed the obvious attachment budding between the boys and their teacher. This concerned him. What if he didn't secure the job as principal? Would he once again uproot the twins? Could he stay in Whispering Slopes and be happy just teaching? He'd worked hard to obtain his master's degree, at the expense of his family. Of course, he needed to focus on keeping his own attachments to Joy in check, too. But that could be difficult since their classrooms would be directly across the hall from each other. He'd never imagined when he'd applied for the open teaching position that she'd be working at the school they'd attended together. One thing he did know: she wasn't going to be happy when she learned he'd be interviewing for the principal position. He couldn't help but wonder if she'd be applying. After all, her father had held the job for most of his career.

"We came to get everything on your list," Tyler called out. He flashed the sheet of paper as the group walked back toward Nick.

Her long brown tresses hung straight to the middle of her back. She quickly tucked a stray strand behind her ear. "I thought you'd stop by after your ice cream. That's why I came."

"You did?" Nick couldn't imagine why she'd want to see him, especially after he'd surprised her earlier at the school. It was obvious she wasn't thrilled to have him back or that she'd be teaching his children. Who could blame her? As far as she knew, he'd never tried to make contact after his father moved their family. But he had. She just didn't know because, unbeknownst to him at the time, his letters had never been mailed. More than anything, he'd wanted to call Joy and explain, but his father didn't want anyone in Whispering Slopes to know their dark secret. Although almost a man, Nick had been torn between his loyalty to his family and his hometown sweetheart. But earlier today, Joy had been a professional and kept her emotions in check in front of Mr. Jacobson. Now, when she looked in his direction, her brow arched, making her look tenser than earlier…if that were possible.

She reached into her camel tote bag and pulled out two red mittens.

"My mittens." Jordan gave a questioning look. "Why do you have them?" He reached inside of his coat pockets.

"I found them on the floor of the coat closet in my classroom."

Nick noticed the tears in his son's eyes. "Are you okay, buddy?"

Jordan's hand shook as he reached for the mittens. "My mommy made these for me," he sniffled. "I'd be sad if I evuh lost them."

"How did you know they belonged to Jordan?" Nick asked, but then he remembered.

"His name is sewn on the inside of each one." Joy looked down at Jordan and smiled. "Obviously your mommy was smart. She knew how easy it is to lose track of these."

Was. The boys had told Joy about their mother.

Jordan slipped his tiny hands inside each mitten. "I'll nevuh forget them again. I pwomise."

Nick rested his hand on his son's shoulder. "I know you won't, Jordan." Although the boy had almost outgrown the garments, Nick knew how special they were to him.

"Let's go check out the candy aisle, Jor!" Tyler motioned for his brother.

Jordan turned to Joy. "Thank you, Miss Kellihuh. I don't know what I would have done if I'd lost these." He gave his teacher a quick hug around the waist and took off toward the treats.

Nick's heart squeezed as he turned to Joy. "Thank you for making a trip over here."

Her smile was warm. "It's on my way home. Besides, we can't have his little fingers freezing. It can get really cold here, especially in the morning when they're headed off for school."

She seemed nervous. He remembered how she used to blink her eyes repeatedly when she was in an uncomfortable situation. "That's thoughtful of you. Speaking of... The boys told me how you helped them get over their first-day-of-school jitters. I appreciate that," he said with hopes of making their encounter a little more comfortable.

"It goes with the territory of being a teacher."

"You're obviously great with children." He glanced at her ring finger, wondering if she'd gotten married, but it was bare. Still, he couldn't help but ask, "No doubt you have several of your own by now?"

He watched as her shoulders stiffened and both brows crinkled.

"I'm sorry... That was rude," he stuttered.

Joy's gaze turned to the boys before looking back in his direction. "So, how are your parents?"

Heat prickled up the back of his neck. Now it was his turn to be uncomfortable. There was so much he wanted to tell her—*needed* to tell her. The reason for his sudden departure...and then the silence on his end. She deserved an explanation, but this wasn't the place. Of course, he wondered if there would ever be the right time or place to tell her. How could he explain how quickly he'd moved on with a new life? "They've both passed on." Nick swallowed hard, in need of a glass of water.

"I'm sorry to hear that—really, I am." She placed her hand on his forearm.

Nick recalled his mother's agonizing death. She'd fought a long battle with her addiction to painkillers—

pills that her doctors handed out like candy following her back injury.

The cuckoo clock hanging behind the counter sounded.

"It was a rough period in my life—those years after my family left." After his mother passed, it got even worse. Watching his father turn to alcohol to mask the pain of losing his partner had been overwhelming for Nick, but it made him realize he had to grow up fast.

"I suppose you have some peace knowing your parents are together with the Lord," she said softly.

That was exactly what had carried him through the most difficult time of his life. Watching his father turn into someone he no longer knew was hard, but then the cancer was discovered in his father's pancreas. It took him fast. He didn't suffer, so that was a blessing. "You're right. My parents are together again."

Following a moment of silence, the twins ran toward the adults.

"Can we go back to the hotel, Daddy? I want to go swimming," Tyler pleaded.

"Hotel?" Joy looked at Nick with an arched brow.

"Yeah, we get to live in a hotel with room service and everything. They even have an indoor pool," Tyler said.

Nick turned at the sound of footsteps pecking across the hardwood floor.

"You can't raise these boys in a hotel," an elderly woman stated.

Sporting the same tight perm, although now snow-white, she looked exactly how he remembered. His heart warmed at the sight of the woman who'd watched him grow up. "Mrs. Buser, it's so nice to see you." He strolled toward her and hugged her tight.

She took a step back, gripping his arms. "Nick Capello,

I knew you'd come back one day." Glancing at the twins, she smiled then returned her attention to him. "Why are you and these cute youngins living in a hotel?"

Joy watched with her arms folded.

"It's only temporary—until our furniture arrives." The moving company had called the day he and the boys were leaving Chicago. They'd promised to have the delivery here in twenty-four hours… That was two days ago. Apparently a bad snowstorm had caused the delay. He made a mental note to call once they were back at the hotel. "I'm sorry—how rude of me. These are my sons, Tyler and Jordan."

The freckled twins smiled at Mrs. Buser. "We like living in the hotel… We don't have to make up the bed." Jordan giggled as his cheeks flushed.

The adults broke out in laughter.

"Come to think of it, *I* could use a week or two in a hotel." The elderly woman tightened the strings on her apron. "Ever since my dear husband passed, I haven't had a moment's rest. But really, I wouldn't have it any other way."

"You should hire some help, Mrs. Buser. At least you could take a day off now and then." Joy voiced her concern.

"I rest on the day of the Lord—that's enough. Besides, running this place has been one of my greatest joys." She glanced at Nick and then Joy. "Seeing the two of you growing up and then falling in love—"

Nick looked toward the boys, relieved to see they had wandered over to the snack aisle.

The elderly woman's face flushed. "I'm sorry. I didn't mean to make either of you uncomfortable." She paused and placed her hand to her heart. "It's just… I always thought you two would get married."

Joy's face reddened as she adjusted her purse strap on her slender shoulder. "Well, I'd better get going. Tell the boys I'll see them in class on Monday."

Before he had a chance to respond, she skidded out the door. Relief settled in when he heard her car pull away. He wanted to talk with her. She deserved an explanation as well as an apology. But not here—not now.

"I'm sorry. I shouldn't have said anything."

The guilt the woman wore on her face caused his heart to squeeze. "Please, don't worry about it. I know people in this town will have a lot of questions about my family's sudden departure and why I've returned," Nick said.

Mrs. Buser rested her warm wrinkled hand on Nick's arm. He turned to her. "Joy is the only person in this town who deserves an explanation. As for the rest of us, it's really none of our business."

Nick swallowed the lump in his throat. "My father loved this town. The hardest thing he ever had to do, apart from burying my mother, was to uproot me and my sister and leave a lot of unanswered questions. He's gone now and it's time for my family to start a new life."

A silence lingered before Mrs. Buser cleared her throat. "So, where do you and the boys plan on living? And your wife?"

"My wife passed away. It's just me and my sons now."

"I'm so sorry."

"I appreciate that. We're doing okay. I found a quaint little house with a wonderful wraparound porch located in Whisper Hill." Before leaving Chicago, Nick had searched available rentals online for several weeks.

He took note of the half smile that parted her lips. "What are you grinning about, Mrs. Buser?"

"Nothing, really—it's just kind of a coincidence."

He scratched his temple. "What is?"

She placed her hand on his forearm. "Why, that's where Joy lives, dear."

Nick couldn't believe his ears. When he'd made the decision to move back to Whispering Slopes, he knew he'd see Joy. She loved this town and the chances of her ever moving away were slim, but never in his wildest of dreams would he have imagined he'd be living so close to his first love. He wanted a new life. It was just him and his boys now, and that was the way it had to remain. He'd had his chance to share his life with someone, but he'd blown it—big-time. He didn't deserve another partner. But didn't his boys deserve the opportunity to grow up with a mother? Should they suffer because of his past mistakes?

Chapter Two

Joy drummed her fingers against the granite countertop, willing her teakettle to hurry up and whistle already. It was Saturday morning and she'd been awake since four o'clock and had already completed her early run. Even a long, hot shower couldn't clear the thoughts of Nick and his boys that had whirled through her head all night. It was bad enough that in two days she'd be working across the hall from Nick, but the news of her first and only love interviewing for the principal position drove her out of her down feather bed. Could Nick take away the only dream she had left, to sit behind the desk in the same office where her father once worked? But more important, a chance to fill the void of being told she'd never have biological children of her own. She'd gone into teaching to be near children—have an impact on their lives, but as principal, she'd have the opportunity to work with and protect all of the children in the school, not only those in her classroom.

The sound of the kettle's whistle pulled her from her thoughts. She needed to keep her focus. Today she had planned to study for the online exam coming up later in the week. She also wanted to do some preparation for her interview. She'd worked hard to earn her master's degree and she was getting closer to fulfilling that goal.

A diesel engine rumbled out front, rattling her porcelain salt and pepper shakers. Joy pushed herself up from the kitchen table and headed toward the bay window in the front of her house. She flipped open the plantation shutters to take a peek. Through the planks she spotted a large truck across the street. The logo that ran along the side of the vehicle read Cross Country Movers.

Moments later a Lexus SUV pulled into the driveway. That must be the new tenant. The Clarks' rental property had been empty for the past six months. She kept her gaze on the vehicle.

Her stomach turned upside down when she spied two identical boys and a caramel-colored puppy bounding from the SUV.

Heat blanketed her face. She raced to her bedroom and yanked on a pair of faded jeans. Stripping off her pink terry cloth robe, she grabbed a wool sweater balled up in her favorite comfy chair. The cold wood floor reminded her she'd need to put on some shoes. Reaching for her running shoes, she jammed her feet inside. Once dressed, she ran a comb through her tangled locks and headed out the front door.

Outside, her feet crunched on the early morning frost as she inhaled the cold air deep into her lungs. She crossed the street and ran up the sidewalk toward the front porch, her heart pounding against her ribs as she took the steps two at a time. She found the front door slightly cracked open, but even in her frantic state, she thought best to knock. "Hello… Anyone in there?"

Giggles sounded through the doorway. "Miss Kelliher!"

Dressed in matching blue-and-white-striped polo sweaters and jeans, the twins skidded to a stop. "How did you know we live here?" Tyler asked as a smile blossomed.

She couldn't have missed the huge truck that rumbled into the neighborhood. "I saw you pull up. My house is right over there." She pointed over her shoulder.

Immediately the boys began to jump up and down, celebrating the fact that they were neighbors.

"This is so awesome! Our favorite teacher ever is right across the street. We can visit you every day!"

Her anger eased as Tyler's words crept inside her wounded heart. But how could she ever live so close to Nick and his boys? A constant reminder of what could have been and what would never be because she was broken…unable to do what should come naturally to a woman—bring new life into the world.

"What's all the commotion?" Nick came up behind his sons, dressed in black jeans and a Northwestern University sweatshirt. As always, he looked startlingly handsome.

Who looks that good when they're moving? Joy's heart fluttered for a split second, until she remembered the reason for her visit. She folded her arms across her chest. "What are you doing here?"

Nick placed his hands on his sons' shoulders. "This is our new home. We're renting now, but the owners are thinking about selling."

This was getting more unbelievable by the second.

"Mrs. Buser mentioned yesterday that we'd be neighbors. I guess it's true what they say about it being a small world." He scratched the side of his head and crinkled his brow.

Neighbors? What was that old saying she'd heard? Good fences made good neighbors—or something like that. That was it… She'd build a fence as high as her homeowners association would allow. She was president—she should know the restrictions. She'd have to check the covenants. Even still, building a wall around her property wouldn't keep Nick out of her heart. "But this is my neighborhood. I moved here after college."

"She lives right over there, Daddy," Tyler announced, pointing in the direction of Joy's one-story ranch home. "Isn't that cool? Maybe she'll invite us over for dinner sometime."

This definitely wasn't cool. Dinner? Absolutely not. How would she avoid Nick when he'd be just outside her door? At that moment she'd give anything to have the old neighbors and their barking Jack Russell back in the house.

"I know I'm probably the last person you want as a neighbor, but we'll just have to make the best of it. This was the only house available that was close to the school."

Right…the school, where he'd be working. "Yes, I suppose the principal wants to be nearby, of course."

Nick's shoulders stiffened. "How did you know I was applying for the position?"

She tilted her head toward the boys. "They mentioned it yesterday while we were out on the playground."

Joy felt a tug on her sweater and looked down at Jordan.

"I'm glad you live so close, Miss Kellihuh." He blushed. "If I get stuck on my homework I can just come ovuh for your help."

Her pulse relaxed when she looked into Jordan's eyes. "You're welcome anytime, sweetie." She turned her attention to Nick. "I'm sorry I came charging over here. I guess I was kind of caught off guard…or maybe I've had too much coffee."

Nick nodded and cleared his throat. "Speaking of coffee, I just started a pot. You must be freezing… Why don't you come inside?"

Practically frozen and not wanting Jordan to think she was still upset, she ignored what her head was telling her and stepped inside. "So you've already unpacked your coffee maker?" She smiled.

"Of course. I have my priorities." Nick winked.

As the two movers scurried past Joy, carrying boxes marked "boys' room," she scanned the open floor plan of the two-story home. She'd only been inside a few times when the previous owners had been out of town and she'd offered to care for their dog.

"Do you want to come see our room, Miss Kelliher?" Tyler reached for her hand. "Daddy bought us bunk beds that look like race cars. They got delivered yesterday while we were at school."

"Let's get that coffee first." Nick headed toward the kitchen.

A whimper sounded behind the closed laundry room door as Joy and the boys trekked toward the aroma of the freshly brewed beverage. "Is that your puppy I hear?"

"How did you know about Maverick?" Jordan asked.

"I saw him when you got out of the car. That's a great name."

"It's from a TV show back in the old days. My daddy likes to watch the reruns." Tyler approached the door.

Joy had a vivid memory of her and Nick on his parents'

sectional sofa, watching old Western movies with an over-size bowl of popcorn sitting between them.

Tyler glanced toward his father. "Is it okay if I let him out, Daddy?"

"Sure—why not? But remember, the movers have the front door opened, so keep an eye on him. We don't want him to run outside without his leash."

Tyler pushed open the door and out sprang a tiny golden nugget of energy. Maverick raced straight to Joy's feet and jumped up and down as though his big paws were springs.

Kneeling down, she extended her hand, which he immediately covered with sloppy, wet kisses. Her heart melted. "He's adorable. What breed is Maverick?"

Nick reached down and stroked the puppy's head. "A labradoodle, and, boy, is he ever a handful. The boys were a little apprehensive when I told them we were moving. I thought Mav would help with the transition."

"He likes you, Miss Kellihuh." Jordan smiled.

Growing up, Joy and Faith had always wanted a dog, but being raised by a grandfather with severe allergies had made that impossible. She scooped Maverick up in her arms and nuzzled his face against her own. "If you ever need a sitter, I'm definitely available." Obviously the adorable fur ball had impaired her thinking. She couldn't pet-sit for the animal. She needed to stay as far away from Nick as possible.

"Excuse me, Mr. Capello, but where would you like the piano?"

The group turned to the short, muscular man standing down the hall.

"How about underneath the window in the living room—is that okay, Jordan?"

The boy nodded. "That's good."

When the mover scurried out the door, Joy turned to Jordan, who seemed more quiet than usual. "Are you the piano player in the family?"

Jordan's cheeks flushed. "Do you think it's only for guls?"

When Tyler silenced a giggle, Joy knew that Jordan had probably been teased about playing the piano. "Of course it's not. There are a lot of well-known pianists who are men. I actually play, too, and I give lessons."

"Weally? My mommy used to play." Jordan glanced at the hardwood floor, looking as if he'd lost his best friend.

Joy noticed Nick's jaw tense. "Boys, we better put Maverick back in the laundry room. We don't want him to get in the movers' way."

Her heart broke for Jordan and Tyler, but also for Nick. One day your life was perfect, complete with a family, and then it was taken from you. Although she wanted to keep her relationship with Nick strictly business, Jordan tugged on her heartstrings. "You just let me know if you'd like for me to give you some lessons." She tipped her thumb under the boy's chin. "I'd better get home. You all have a lot of unpacking to do. Besides, I've had enough coffee this morning. I'll see you all on Monday."

As she walked toward her empty home, thoughts of the two freckle-faced boys and the rambunctious puppy flooded her mind. Nick's family. Her heart squeezed. It was as though she was seeing a flash of her life as it could have been. It would have been a wonderful life. When she reached for the icy doorknob on her empty home, she couldn't help but wonder if it would be that easy to keep things on a professional level.

Nick watched Joy through the front window as she headed back to her home—directly across the street from his own. What were the odds? He should have found out where she lived in Whispering Slopes before making the move. Of course, it was too late now. For better or worse they were going to be neighbors and he'd just have to do the best he could to keep his distance. With the boys and Maverick it could prove to be a challenge, but he was determined to make a fresh start for his family.

He gazed around their new home and smiled. The oversize living room would serve as the family room, where they'd watch television, play games and enjoy being together. Something he hadn't made much time for while living and teaching in Chicago. That would change. He might not deserve the opportunity to be a better husband, but he sure would be the best father for his boys.

Nick released a slow and easy breath. He'd made the right decision by moving here, hadn't he? But one thing he hadn't expected when he packed up their old house in Chicago was for all the guilt he carried about his wife to make the move with him. Silly. Why would he think a new location could erase the past?

"Daddy?"

Nick turned to see Jordan standing behind him. He reached for his son's hand and guided him toward the sofa the movers had placed in the living room earlier. "What is it, son?" he asked, lifting his boy up on his lap. His stomach knotted realizing soon the time would come where moments like this would become a distant memory.

"Do you think it would be okay if I asked Miss Kelli-huh to give me piano lessons?"

Nick couldn't help but notice the hesitation in Jordan's question. "Why do you think there'd be anything wrong with that?"

The little boy bit down on his quivering lower lip. "Well, since Mommy used to teach me, I didn't know if she'd like that. I wouldn't want to disappoint huh."

Nick's heart ached for his son. At the age of three, Jordan had been drawn to the piano like a hummingbird to fresh nectar. Whenever his mother had played, he'd toddle to her side. She'd lift him up on the bench and he'd listen while she played. He'd giggle when she played "Three Blind Mice" and get sleepy when she'd play the soothing sound of "Brahms's Lullaby." Although self-taught, his wife, Michelle, had a natural talent to create beautiful melodies.

"I think it would make your mother really proud to know you want to continue learning how to play her favorite instrument."

Jordan squirmed in his father's lap before resting his head against Nick's chest. "I miss huh, Daddy." He wiped away a stray tear that escaped from his sad eyes. "Will I always feel this way?"

The million-dollar question—Nick had asked himself this daily. Some days were tougher than others, but the sadness cast a shadow over his heart that never seemed to fade. "I think we'll always miss her, but one day, it won't hurt as much. Maybe we'll be able to think of your mommy and smile as we remember the good times we had with her." Nick wondered how soon that day would arrive.

Early Monday morning, Nick and the boys snaked their way through the line inside of the school's cafeteria. A free breakfast was available to each student, if they didn't have time to eat at home or if money was tight for the family. This was a program Nick fully endorsed. He firmly believed that students were more focused when they started their day with a healthy breakfast. He had to admit, though, there was something special about cooking the morning meal for his boys in the comfort of their home.

"Can I have a doughnut, Daddy?"

Not exactly the meal he wanted for his sons. "Yes, but I want you to eat some eggs and fruit first."

Tyler crinkled his nose before scooping some scrambled eggs onto his plate.

The sounds of children chattering filled the room. Nick had missed being in a school. After his wife passed away, he'd taken a leave of absence from his teaching position. It felt good to be back in this environment. This was where he belonged.

With their trays loaded, Nick and the twins headed toward an empty table next to a window. The bright sunlight beamed across the room, providing some added warmth—a perfect winter day.

Jordan took a bite of his banana and his eyes popped. "Look—there's Miss Kellihuh!"

"Who's that with her, Daddy?" Tyler eyed the little girl holding Joy's hand.

"I'm not sure." Nick turned and watched Joy glide across the room. She smiled, stopping at each table to greet the children.

"Miss Kellihuh! Come sit with us," Jordan shouted.

Nick took note of Jordan's uncharacteristic outburst. It was unusual for him to want to draw attention to himself. His face exploded with happiness as he bounced up and down in his chair.

Dressed in black pants and a white angora sweater, Joy approached their table. Her hair was twisted into a bun with a few loose tendrils framing her face. "Good morning, boys. This is my niece, Bella Carlson." She turned to the twins. "Bella, this is Jordan and Tyler."

"Twins—cool!" Bella stepped closer. "My mommy and Aunt Joy are twins."

"That's cool, too," Tyler said.

"Bella, this is Mr. Capello. He'll be your new teacher, since he's taking over Mrs. Murray's class while she's out on maternity leave."

Nick extended his hand. "It's nice to meet you, Bella."

"You're tall." Bella giggled.

Joy glanced at the twins' plates. "Are you both eating a nice healthy breakfast?"

"I'm having eggs and a doughnut for dessert," Tyler answered before taking another bite.

"Can you guys come and sit with us?" Jordan asked in a hushed tone. "I wanted to ask you something, Miss Kellihuh."

Joy glanced toward Nick as if to seek his approval.

Nick stood and pulled out the empty chair. "Yes, please, join us."

Bella took the vacant seat next to Tyler. Joy settled in the chair next to Nick and folded her hands together before placing them on the table. A sweet fragrance tickled his nose.

Joy leaned toward Jordan. "What is it you wanted to ask me, sweetie?"

Nick watched as his son's cheeks flushed before he glanced down toward the ground and then quickly looked at his teacher. "Do you think you could give me piano lessons?"

"Well… I suppose that would be okay." She turned to Nick. "Would it be all right with you?"

Until he received an offer for the principal position, he'd prefer for his boys to have as little interaction with Joy as possible outside of school, but he knew how happy it would make Jordan. Although both boys missed their mother, Jordan seemed to be having a more difficult time coping with her death. It was no wonder he'd become attached to Joy so quickly. And why wouldn't he? She was compassionate and she obviously loved the children. He couldn't help but wonder if she wanted children of her own one day.

Nick nodded. "Yes. We discussed it already. We will certainly work around your schedule, and of course, you'll be compensated fairly." He'd keep it strictly a business relationship and somehow find a way to make himself scarce while she gave Jordan his lessons.

"Yippee! Thank you, Miss Kellihuh." Jordan jumped from his chair and hugged Joy around her waist.

Nick's heart tightened. His son longed for a mother figure. But Jordan's father had failed once at being a husband. Did he deserve a second chance?

Three hours later, Nick had completed his morning lessons. While his class was outside for recess, he headed to the teachers' lounge for a much-needed cup of coffee.

The accent lamps on each round table provided a warm glow, rather than the bright fluorescent lighting that filled the school. It was an inviting atmosphere. Two teachers occupied a table in the corner but neither looked up as he stepped inside, so he strolled in silence to the coffee bar.

Normally, he'd stop to talk with his fellow coworkers, but the twosome appeared to be involved in a heated political discussion. That was a topic he avoided talking about with friends and fellow teachers. He filled a large mug with the piping hot brew before adding a splash of cream. Giving it three quick stirs, he scanned the room and decided to take the table near the window that looked out onto the playground.

He settled into the chair and reached for his backpack. He planned to use his break to do some preparing for his upcoming interview. Glancing out the window, he smiled when he saw his boys taking turns pushing Bella on the swing. She was a sweet little girl who he believed would have a positive influence on Jordan and Tyler.

Moments later, the sound of footsteps tapping along the tiled floor took his attention from his notes. Joy made eye contact, gave a half smile, but then quickly looked away and headed to an empty table across from where he sat.

Nick wasn't surprised by her reaction. The circumstances surrounding his sudden departure had upset her. He got that, but they still had to work together. Plus, she'd be giving Jordan piano lessons. He owed her an explanation so they could try to move forward and put the past behind them.

He exhaled a deep breath and pushed away from the table. As he approached Joy, she never looked his way. Maybe she thought he was going back for more coffee.

"Joy?"

She flinched, appearing startled by his presence. "I'm sorry. I didn't know you were standing there." She closed the notebook resting on the table.

"You saw me when you came in. Why didn't you come over?"

"I apologize. I've got a lot on my mind."

"I'm sure you do, and no doubt a lot of it has to do with my return to town." The last thing in the world he wanted to do was to cause her more pain. "With us teaching across the hall from each other and living in the same neighborhood, it's obvious we're going to be seeing a lot of each other."

Joy looked up and caught his gaze. "Don't forget I'll be teaching your son how to play the piano, too."

Nick pulled out a chair. "Do you mind if I sit for a minute?"

She shrugged her shoulders.

Since her shrug was more than she'd given him earlier, he took a seat. "I wanted to thank you for agreeing to teach Jordan. He's really excited."

A smile parted her lips. "He's a sweet boy, Nick. He'll do well with lessons. He's the perfect student—eager to learn."

"The piano is special to him for many reasons, so thanks." He started to get up from the table, but then slid back into the chair. "For what it's worth, I wanted to call you after my family left. You might not believe me, but it's the truth. My father didn't want me to have any contact with friends from Whispering Slopes. It's a long story and one I hope to share with you, but he did it to protect my mother. I wrote to you. But when you didn't answer, I assumed you were too upset with me and had moved on. Years later, I learned from my father that he'd intercepted all of my letters from the mailbox, so they were never delivered to you."

Joy slid her notebook into her bag. "I can't talk about this here, Nick. Please, let's forget everything that happened in the past. It will make things much easier."

The pain in her eyes was more than he could bear.

"Will it? Do you really think pretending we don't have a history will make things right again?" He ran his hand down the side of his cleanly shaven face.

"No, but if we're going to maintain our professionalism, I don't think we have a choice." She stood from her chair and reached for her bag. "Oh, I almost forgot. Rehearsal will begin tomorrow afternoon. We'll practice on Tuesdays and Thursdays."

His left brow arched. "What are we rehearsing?"

"Didn't Mr. Jacobson talk with you earlier?"

Nick shook his head. "I haven't seen him this morning."

"He wants the first- and second-grade classes to perform a play together for the school's talent week—*Little Red Riding Hood*." She turned on her heel and glided out the door as a soft floral fragrance trailed behind her.

Nick took note of the time and headed to his table to grab his things. A play—with her class? Unbelievable. It was as though God was doing everything in His power to throw them together. Had He orchestrated this second chance for Nick and Joy?

Chapter Three

Tuesday afternoon, Joy sat in the third row of the school's auditorium. The students had been released from school and those participating in the play were outside enjoying a brief recess with the teaching assistants before rehearsal. Earlier in the day, she'd received an email from Nick requesting they meet privately before the first rehearsal. Her stomach fluttered as she wondered what he wanted to talk about. Of course, in her heart she knew. The past. Something she'd like to bury deep inside the earth's core. Until his return to Whispering Slopes, she'd done a pretty good job at covering up her secret, but that hadn't kept it from festering like a cut that wouldn't heal.

Decisions have consequences. Growing up, that was what her grandmother always told her. Her decision the night she waited for Nick by the pond had forever changed her as a person. How could she ever share this with Nick?

The squeak of the door from the back of the room announced his arrival. She swallowed hard and turned. He strolled down the aisle of the auditorium dressed in khaki relaxed-fit pants and a red pullover sweater. That was always his color. It looked great with his close-cut dark hair. She pushed out of the wooden chair and braced herself.

"Thanks for meeting me." He shoved his hands into his pockets. "Since we're going to be working so closely together on the play, I thought it would be a good idea to clear the air."

"That's an interesting metaphor. From what I recall of the night, you didn't show up. There's no misunderstanding in that."

"You're right." He motioned toward the chairs. "Can we sit down and talk?"

She sounded defensive—she knew that—but what choice did she have? If she let down her guard, he'd find out everything. She couldn't allow that to happen. "I'm listening."

Nick leaned back in the chair and crossed his right leg over his left knee. "Do you remember when my mother fell down the stairs and injured her back?" he asked with his hands clasped together.

Joy's thoughts drifted to that late autumn afternoon. The two of them had been studying at the dining room table when they heard a thumping sound and then cries for help. They'd raced into the foyer and had discovered his mother at the bottom of the stairs, the contents of the laundry basket strewn all over the pinewood floor. She couldn't move.

"Yes, I remember. She went to the hospital for several weeks. Didn't she have two or three surgeries?"

"Yes, three." He nodded. "Unfortunately, the surgeries didn't give her any relief from the excruciating pain she lived with on a daily basis."

Last year, while lifting some heavy boxes in her classroom, Joy had strained her back. The pain she'd experienced lasted for several days. She couldn't imagine the ongoing pain Mrs. Capello must have dealt with. "That's terrible… I had no idea."

"No one really did. She stayed isolated in her room for months. Although she was the one in tremendous pain, it also took a heavy toll on my father and their marriage."

"I'm sure it was hard on everyone…including yourself."

Nick nodded. "Her doctor kept prescribing higher doses of pain medications. The more she took, the more she needed. One night, I was in bed and I heard her crying through the wall. My father had been out of town on business, so I got up to check on her. I'll never forget the look of despair blanketing her face." He paused and raked his hand across the back of his neck. "When I asked her if she needed anything she told me she wanted it all to end."

Her stomach twisted. Mrs. Capello was such a sweet and loving woman. She'd opened her home to Joy and treated her like a daughter. Joy had grown up without a mother of her own, and the woman's kindness had always meant so much to her.

"I'm so sorry, Nick. I wish you'd told me how bad things were."

"I almost did—a couple of times. But in a way, spending time with you was an escape from the trouble at home. I wanted to keep it that way and not bring my problems into our relationship."

"Yes, but healthy relationships involve sharing problems with each other." Of course, she could never reveal the events that occurred after he'd left.

He leaned forward and turned toward her. "Believe me, that's a lesson I've learned much too late in life."

Joy's eyebrows arched. It sounded as though there was

more about his past she didn't know—just like he didn't know about her own. Perhaps that was all for the best.

"Anyway, that's the reason why he moved us—to protect my mother. The abuse of painkillers got more out of control and she'd threatened to hurt herself several times. My father reached out to a friend of his from college who worked as an addiction specialist practicing in Chicago. He offered to accept my mother into a new study program. It started the following week. We left on a Friday night and she was admitted on Monday. She stayed at the facility for six months."

How could she be upset? His father had loved his mother and had no other options. Still, Nick never came back for her—the wound was still raw.

He reached for her hand. "Once I found out the letters had never been sent, it was too late. My circumstances had changed."

All she could do was nod and pull her hand away. *Let him talk, but keep your distance.* She couldn't allow herself to get close to him again. He was back to steal her dream. Besides, everything had changed and she'd never want him to know that she wasn't like most women.

"My father's reputation in the community was important to him. He cared what people thought about him and his family. He didn't want others to look down on his wife or him."

"You could have trusted me. I wouldn't have said anything to anyone." Even as she spoke the words, an understanding of Mr. Capello's reasons settled in. She had secrets of her own she wanted to keep buried.

"I know, but my father didn't. His mind wasn't in the right place back then, and he wanted to protect her privacy."

"After the six months, did your mother recover?" He could have come back to her then.

He ran his hand down the side of his face. "You're wondering why I didn't return after she finished rehab, aren't you?"

Her left brow arched.

"In the beginning, since I didn't know my letters were never mailed, I assumed you never wanted to talk to me again. I was afraid to come back and discover that you'd moved on—maybe married and started a family with someone else…someone other than me." He pulled his eyes off her and stared at the ground. "After I promised to spend my life with you, I abandoned you. You had every right to move on, but I guess I just didn't want to know if you had. Then I met the boys' mother, and, well…too much time passed."

If only he knew. Any chance of a relationship with anyone had ended that night. She'd been betrayed on so many different levels. How could she ever trust another man? But really, what did it matter? No man would ever want her now.

She swallowed to loosen the lump lodged in her throat. "I appreciate you telling me why you left. If you don't want to talk about it anymore, I understand."

Sadness pooled in his eyes. "No, you asked about her recovery. After the treatment, she was good for a year or so. When her back problems returned, she went to a new doctor. Just like the others, he overprescribed pills. Once again, she was in and out of rehab. I was relieved to be away at college, although I felt bad I wasn't there to support my father and my sister, Janie. It was just too hard. I had to get out of that house and build a life for myself with Michelle. That's her name—*was* her name. I tried to come home from school as much as I could, but it was too painful to see what had happened to my family. Janie tried to help our dad, but she really struggled after our mother passed. Then my father slipped into a deep depression." He paused and exhaled a heavy breath. "I suggested counseling, but he didn't see the point. When my mother's kidneys started to fail due to the years of drug abuse, I actually prayed for God to take her. She'd given up on life years before. The only hope my father had of salvaging his life was if he no longer felt responsible for her."

Joy had no words. She wished she'd known. Perhaps there would have been something she could have done to help the Capello family. If she had, would both of their lives have turned out differently?

He ran his hand through his hair. "It's hard to believe. Sometimes it feels like a lifetime ago, but other times, if feels like yesterday."

"The pain still feels new," Joy added.

He caught her gaze and held it. "Exactly. I suppose that's how it feels for you."

She remained silent.

"After my mother died, things got worse for my father. He started to drink heavily. Then he was diagnosed with pancreatic cancer and passed away within a few months."

"I'm sorry, Nick…really, I am. He was a good man."

The two sat in silence for the next five minutes. "I need a little air before the children come inside from recess," she said.

He nodded. "I think I'll go and grab a quick cup of coffee."

Once outside, her thoughts drifted to Nick's father. The poor man had lived a life full of constant heartache and pain. She couldn't help but wonder if she was headed down that same road.

After sipping his beverage in the teachers' lounge and receiving a phone call from a friend in Chicago, Nick inhaled a deep breath before entering the school's auditorium. Part of him was relieved he'd spoken to Joy and told her why his family had left town, but something told him she had secrets she was holding on to as well. Her eyes had a sadness that didn't exist when they were younger.

"Daddy! We've been waiting for you." Tyler raced to the door and flung his arms around Nick's waist.

He spotted Joy up on the stage, laughing with a group of children. She looked radiant.

"I'm sorry—I got held up on a call." He took his son's hand and strolled down the aisle.

"I sure hope I get picked to play the Big Bad Wolf," Tyler declared.

Nick stepped up on the stage. "I'm late—sorry," he said to Joy, who appeared busy scribbling notes on a clipboard. With her hair now pulled back in a ponytail, she reminded him of the young girl he'd fallen in love with. He shook off the thought. Their relationship was anything but the same. It could never be more. Besides, now they were just rivals.

"No worries. I was letting the kids know there are many other parts besides the leads. We need to cast the animals, trees, mushrooms, and we'll also need help with costumes and lighting."

Tyler stepped forward. "What about the wolf, Miss Kelliher? You forgot about that."

Nick couldn't help but notice Joy's smile fading.

"What's wrong, Joy?"

"Nothing. I'm fine."

She didn't look fine. Her voice shook and she appeared pale.

"So, raise your hand if you'd like to play the wolf," Nick called, scanning the group for volunteers.

"First, we have to cast the lead," Joy said.

He didn't want to argue with her. "Okay, so who wants to play Little Red Riding Hood?"

When no hands went up, Nick looked at Bella. "I think you'd be perfect in the role."

Her cheeks flushed. "Are you sure?" Bella asked in a less-than-confident tone.

"I'm positive. What about you, Miss Kelliher? Don't you agree?"

Joy smiled. "I think she'd be perfect."

Bella kicked her tennis shoe against the wooden stage. "What if I can't learn all my lines?"

"I can help you." Tyler stepped forward.

Nick smiled at his son. He always liked to help others. "I think that's a good idea, Tyler." He glanced at Bella. "You'll do great, so don't worry."

"Can I play the wolf, Daddy?" Tyler tugged on Nick's arm.

"We have to give everyone an opportunity, son. If there are others interested we'll have to conduct some tryouts. Do you agree, Mrs. Kelliher?"

Joy nodded. "It only seems fair," she answered before turning her attention back to the clipboard.

Nick couldn't help wondering why Joy seemed so disengaged. He knew she loved the children, but something told me she wasn't into this play. He pointed to the far side of the stage. "Anyone who'd like the role of the wolf, please step over there."

Tyler skipped across the floor, making it clear he was interested, but he was the only one.

Nick glanced over the group of children, all of whom stared at the ground, unresponsive. "Okay, then. Tyler, by default, it looks like you've got the part."

"Yippee!" His son ran toward Joy. "Did you hear, Miss Kelliher? I get to be the wolf."

"Yes, I heard… Congratulations." She quickly turned her attention to her clipboard again.

An hour and a half later the children had been picked up by their parents. While the twins and Bella acted out various routines on the stage, Nick was alone with Joy for the second time this afternoon. Sitting in the middle of the auditorium, they mapped out their rehearsal calendar for the next week.

"With the play scheduled in a few weeks, Mr. Jacobson isn't giving us much time to practice, is he?" Nick glanced at Joy, who only nodded. She'd said very little to him since the children had gone home. He'd noticed she'd been less than enthusiastic about Tyler's part in the play.

"So, I take it you're not really an admirer of the Big Bad Wolf." He turned in her direction. "I don't really remember you being afraid when we were kids," he joked.

Her shoulders stiffened. "What makes you say that?" She fingered her gold chain.

"I don't know. It seems like you got a little tense earlier whenever he was mentioned."

"I just wish Mr. Jacobson would have picked another fairy tale, that's all." She stared toward the stage.

Nick thought best to change the subject. For some

reason she wasn't a fan of "Little Red Riding Hood," but hey, he never cared for "Rapunzel."

"I wanted to apologize if Jordan put you in an uncomfortable position yesterday by asking about the piano lessons."

"Of course he didn't. I had offered, remember?" Joy removed her reading glasses and placed them on top of her head. "Are you okay with it?"

Nick worked his jaw back and forth. "I want Jordan to be happy."

"You seemed somewhat agitated the other morning when he brought up his mother and the lessons. Do you ever talk to the boys about her?"

He knew he hadn't been a good husband, but now he was a bad father. Was that what she was implying?

Nick squirmed in his seat. "I don't want to talk about this now."

Joy blew out a breath. "That could be a big part of your problem."

What? Did he have a problem when it came to his boys? He didn't think so. "I'm not understanding, Joy."

"Your son needs to express his feelings. You need to open the door for conversations with Jordan and Tyler. It's important they're allowed to talk about their mother."

Nick felt cornered. She did think he was a bad father. "The last time I looked, you weren't a parent, Joy. So please, don't lecture me on how to talk with my sons."

The murmurs of the children on stage seeped into Nick's ears as Joy remained silent. As soon as he'd spoken the words, regret washed over him. "I'm sorry... That was a low blow."

Joy folded her arms tight around her body. "No, you're right. I don't have children of my own, but I do have experience with those who have had tragedy in their life. Any professional will tell you that brushing it under the rug and ignoring the incident won't make it go away. It's not too late, Nick—trust me."

"But what if it is?" It was certainly too late for him and his wife. How would Joy react if she found out the truth… that his own children had known their mother was sick, but he hadn't? Or had he chosen to ignore it? How pathetic.

Nick flinched when he felt the tender touch of her hand on his own.

"Please, don't do this to yourself, Nick. You can't change the past, but moving forward, you can do things differently."

He fought back the tears attempting to release. "I don't even know where to begin. Sometimes when I see the boys watching their friends with their mothers, the pain in their eyes makes me feel like the worst father in the world." This was exactly the reason why he had to get the job of principal—all of his time invested back in Chicago, studying and pushing himself at the expense of his family, would have been for nothing if he couldn't advance his career.

"You can begin by just talking to them and reminiscing about your wife. When I was their age, I loved when my grandmother and grandfather would tell me and Faith stories about our parents. It made the pain of losing them more bearable. Plus, since we'd been so young when they died, hearing about them made my mother and father more real…if that makes sense."

The two sat in silence for a few minutes as they watched Bella and the boys dancing around on the stage.

"Yes, it does." Nick cleared his throat and turned toward Joy. "I apologize for dumping all of that on you, but I think I'm beginning to see your point."

"And what's that?"

"Well, I feel a little better talking with you, so maybe if I try it with Jordan and Tyler, they'll start to feel good, too."

Joy laughed. "I promise you, it will help, but as for an apology, it's not necessary. You've suffered a tremendous loss and raising children on your own can't be easy."

It was the hardest thing he'd ever done apart from burying his wife. "Well, I won't lie—it's not, but having good friends helps. Jordan and I would really like for you to go ahead with the lessons."

A smile parted her lips. "I'd like that, too. It's nice to see a child interested in music at such a young age."

"His interest is all Michelle's doing. She loved the piano and encouraged both boys to play. Tyler just didn't have any interest. He prefers any sport that involves a ball over music." Nick smiled.

"When I become principal, I'd really like to expand the music department," Joy said. "I think it supports all learning. I've read studies that indicate musical training can physically develop the left portion of the brain. That's the side involved with processing language." She removed her glasses from her head and slid them on when her phone pinged.

Nick wasn't sure if he'd heard her clearly or not. "What? You're interviewing for the position?"

Joy forced a laughed. "Of course I am. I had assumed you already knew. In fact, according to Mr. Jacobson, I'm your only competition. It's been my dream to fill my father's shoes by becoming principal. I've been preparing for this job for years. Plus, it won't be long before I have my master's degree."

"Well, I already have a master's." Nick pushed his shoulders back.

"That's a nonissue."

He shook his head. "Probably not to the school board when they're determining who is better qualified to hold the job."

"I'll have it before the end of May," she declared as she sprang to her feet with a face the color of a summertime cherry. "I think we're done here. I've got to get Bella home for dinner." She hugged her purse close to her stomach.

Nick sat in the chair as he watched Joy march down the aisle of the auditorium. Taking the steps two at a time, she reached for Bella's hand and exited the platform faster than an actor with stage fright.

He shook his head. He should have known better and kept his mouth shut. A few minutes earlier, he thought maybe they could be friends again and move on from the past. If he was honest with himself, there was nothing he wanted more. But that ship had sailed long ago. Actually…sunk was more like it. But he'd come back to Whispering Slopes for a new start for him and his boys. One way or another, he'd eventually right this ship, but in the meantime, he knew there'd be plenty of choppy waters ahead, especially with both competing for the principal position. One thing he knew for sure: he was determined to get this job. Otherwise, all of the long hours and hard work he'd put into obtaining his advanced degree would have been for nothing. But then again, getting this job wouldn't change the past and bring back Michelle.

Chapter Four

Late Thursday afternoon, Joy lit the cinnamon-scented candle resting on the countertop and resumed pacing the travertine tile of her kitchen floor. Anticipating the arrival of her guests, her eyes were glued on the front window. Earlier this morning, when she'd asked Nick what he and the boys were contributing to the school bake sale tomorrow and his face had gone blank, she'd known he'd missed the email. Feeling sorry for him, she'd extended the invitation to him and the twins to come over so they could all bake together. She had to admit, at first a sense of excitement had fluttered in her heart, but now her stomach felt like rubber balls were bouncing inside—maybe because her only contender for the principal job happened to be the most handsome man she'd ever known and the only one who ever made her feel safe.

The past two days, rehearsing with Nick had proved to be more of a challenge than she had anticipated and the choice of plays certainly wasn't helping. When Mr. Jacobson suggested *Little Red Riding Hood*, a shiver had run down Joy's spine. As a child, she'd been frightened by this fairy tale. After her grandmother had read the story to her and Faith for the first time, she'd checked underneath her bed every night for weeks. Eventually, she told Mamaw she'd rather not hear the story again. Now, as an adult, she had her own real-life "big bad wolf" who continued to haunt her dreams, so many years later. Scotty—the star quarterback. Although she hadn't seen him since graduation, he'd taken up a permanent space in her memory. She had a feeling Nick had sensed something from her during rehearsal on Tuesday and today. She'd have to make an extra effort to keep her emotions under wraps, otherwise her secret could blow wide-open.

"What's the matter, Aunt Joy?" Bella tugged on Joy's silk crepe blouse and gazed up with doe-like eyes that never failed to melt her heart.

No. She wouldn't let her mind wander down that road—not now when she was expecting company. She had to keep her focus and not allow any of those old memories to take hold and ruin everyone's evening.

"Nothing's wrong."

Bella giggled. "You've been looking out that window forever."

"I want to make sure I hear our guests when they arrive."

"Won't they ring the doorbell?"

Her shoulders relaxed, but only for a second. "You're right—they will." She'd been relieved when Bella had asked if they could bake together since her mother usually burned the cookies. Her niece and the twins would serve as a good buffer between her and Nick tonight. "What do you say we do a few pieces of the jigsaw puzzle I started on the dining room table?"

Bella skipped toward the other room. "I love puzzles. Maybe Tyler and Jordan will want to help."

"Maybe." Joy took another peek before joining her niece.

Ten minutes later the bell rang. Joy's stomach rolled over like a dog hoping for a good belly scratch.

"They're here, they're here." Bella sprang from her chair and raced toward the front door.

Joy followed behind, straightening her hair with one hand and then the other and questioning why she'd ever extended the invitation. She sucked in a deep breath—it was too late now.

Bella jerked the door open and Joy's heart raced when she saw Nick and his boys on the porch, holding a bunch of forget-me-nots. Her favorite flower and the first he'd ever given her when they were thirteen years old. Nick's father had driven her and his son on their first of many dates to One More Scoop. That night, two nervous teenagers had shared their first kiss.

"Hi, Bella! Hi, Miss Kelliher!" the boys sang out as they stepped into the foyer.

"Look what my daddy bwought for you." Jordan smiled.

Bella turned to her aunt. "Those are your favorite."

Nick handed his cluster to Joy. His face reddened. "I remembered."

A fiery heat prickled the back of her neck. How did he remember? It had been so long ago. Her heart ached for a second until she recalled how their story had ended. She reached out for the flowers. "How thoughtful— thank you." She accepted all three clusters and walked down the hallway toward the kitchen pantry. "Please, come in and make yourself comfortable. I'm going to put these in some water."

"I'll take your coats," Bella offered. "Do you want to help with our jigsaw puzzle before we start baking?"

"Sure!" the twins answered.

"Come on, Daddy." The boys tugged on their father's arm.

The two adults eyed each other.

"You go ahead, kids. I'll be in in just a couple of minutes," Nick said as the children scurried from the room, giggling and whispering.

With a shaky hand, Joy turned on the faucet and slid the vase underneath the stream of water. The sound of footsteps on the hardwood approached from behind.

"I'm sorry if I made you uncomfortable."

She gripped the brushed copper handle, shut off the water and turned to face him. "What do you mean?"

"The flowers—I remembered how happy they'd made you the first time I gave them to you. I just thought… Well, maybe it was a bad idea."

Joy's emotions swirled like fresh snowflakes caught up in a gusty breeze. "I can't do this, Nick."

"What?"

She ran her hands down the front of her jeans. "I can't take a trip down memory lane with you." She needed to keep her memories at bay. Going down that road would lead her to the night she'd tried so hard to forget. Now, fourteen years later, the event flashed through her mind as though it were yesterday, and she was standing in her kitchen with the only person who could have saved her that horrible night.

A look of disappointment blanketed his face. "There's no motive behind me buying flowers for you and Bella. It's just a thank-you for helping me and the boys out— you know, with the baking. I'm sorry if it upset you."

If only bringing her wildflowers could erase the past, but that only happened in fairy tales. "Let's forget it. We're here for the children. We don't want to ruin the evening for them by dredging up the past."

Three hours and eight dozen cookies later, both the kitchen floor and the children were a mess. Joy had decided to forgo her obsession with neatness. She wanted the kids to have a little fun. In the end, a battle broke out with handfuls of flour tossed in every direction. Even she and Nick had joined in. She couldn't remember the last time her house had been filled with so much laughter. Who was she kidding? Without a family of her own to fill the rooms, her house was typically silent. Several times she'd caught Nick staring at her with the dreamy smile that had first captured her heart.

"Don't worry—I'll help you clean up this mess. I remember how you like everything in order." Nick's lips parted into an easy smile, causing Joy's heart to beat a tiny bit faster.

"Are you saying I'm a neat freak?"

He laughed. "You said it… I didn't."

With the cookies baked and wrapped up for the sale tomorrow, the children had gone back to the jigsaw puzzle in the other room. Joy busied herself wiping down the granite countertops with a warm dishcloth.

Nick slowly approached the opposite side of the island and placed his hand over hers. She wanted to pull away, but it was like a magnetic force. That was the way their relationship had always been. They could never spend a moment apart from one another—until they were left with no choice.

"I wanted to apologize for how I acted on Tuesday, after rehearsal." His crystal eyes shimmered under the pendant lighting. "My comment to you about not having children was completely out of line and totally insensitive."

Finally breaking their connection, she pulled her hand away and stuffed it into the pocket of her jeans, safe from his warm touch. The subject of children was off-limits, as it would only result in Nick learning the truth of why she didn't have any of her own. And then what? His pity... That was the last thing she needed or wanted. "It's already been forgotten." She squirmed at her own fib.

Nick mauled his unshaven chin with his hand. "Since losing Michelle, trying to do what's best for the boys has been my number one priority, but many times I think I've been putting myself first by not talking to them about their mother. It's easier to brush my own mistakes under the rug by avoiding the topic altogether."

Joy completely understood how Nick felt when it came to talking about his wife with the boys. After all, she was the queen of brushing issues under the carpet. Even so, despite all that had happened in their past, her heart ached for his situation. Some of her previous students had fathers raising children on their own, so she knew the challenges. "Don't be so hard on yourself. I'm sure you're doing the best you can."

Outside, a coyote's howl broke the silence that hung in the air.

"I haven't heard that sound in years. We didn't have a lot of coyotes in Chicago."

"Do you miss it—the city?" Joy couldn't imagine living in a large metropolitan area. Whispering Slopes cradled her like a safe cocoon.

Nick shook his head. "Not in the least. My heart has always belonged to the Shenandoah Valley. After I married Michelle I tried to talk her into moving back here, but she was a city girl...born and raised."

Joy was relieved he hadn't come back with his new wife. Back then, she never would have been strong enough to witness Nick with another woman. Not to mention seeing him start a family. Even now, with so many years behind them, watching him with children was a perpetual reminder of what could have been and a more scorching pain of what would never be.

Nick observed Joy as she busied herself at the kitchen sink. She looked as beautiful as he remembered, except an ever-present sadness in her eyes had replaced the sparkle that was once there. Since he'd returned to Whispering Slopes, he couldn't help but wonder what his life—their life together—would have been like if he hadn't been forced to leave. He knew he couldn't keep torturing himself with the what-ifs. *It is what it is.* Wasn't that what everyone said? Personally, he never liked that saying.

"I suppose we should order the pizza now."

Joy's words pulled him back into the moment.

"Sounds good—I'm starved. I might have to talk with Faith and Joshua about hiring out Bella. I don't think I've ever heard the boys this quiet." His chair scratched along the hardwood floor as he rose from the table.

Joy wiped her hand on a checkered dish towel and flung it onto the kitchen counter. "We'd better go check on them."

As the adults entered the dining room, the children had their heads buried in the scattered puzzle pieces.

"Come see how much we've done, Daddy," Jordan

said, tearing his eyes away from their masterpiece, but only for a second.

Joy took a seat next to her niece while Nick slipped into the last empty chair in between Bella and Tyler. Outside, a gust of wind rattled the windowpanes.

"You kids work well together." Nick smiled, happy to see his sons enjoying themselves.

"Hey, we should be a team for the snowman making at the winter festival," Bella chirped.

"What's that?" Tyler looked up from the puzzle.

Joy glanced at Nick. "You've seen the emails, haven't you?"

Since his first day, he's been scrolling through page upon page of messages sent through the school's email system. He couldn't recall receiving this many back in Chicago. Truth be told, he was having a difficult time keeping up with all of them. Obviously he needed to do a better job at that. Never big on some of the advances in technology, he preferred face-to-face conversations and handwritten letters over email. "I don't think I have."

"Well, the winter festival is mandatory for all teachers. They expect our attendance since it's sponsored by the school. It's a good way for the teachers to show the kids they know how to have fun, too," Joy explained. "It's a week from this Saturday."

"Don't worry, Mr. Nick—you'll have fun. It's at our inn, the Black Bear. There's going to be pony rides, downhill ski races, sleigh rides…everything!" Bella turned toward the twins. "So do you want to pair up? Every team gets to pick a charity and Buser's General Store is going to donate five thousand dollars for the winning team. I think Mrs. Buser is rich." Bella giggled.

"We picked the Crohn's and Colitis Foundation for our donations because of Sherida."

The twins' heads pivoted toward Nick. "Can we go, Daddy? Please..."

Before Michelle had gotten sick, he'd never heard of the disease. Now someone close to Joy was living with it. Was this God's way of making sure he didn't forget what a bad husband he'd been? Nick looked toward his excited boys then turned to Joy. "Who's Sherida?"

"She's Faith and Joshua's marketing director and their first official hire when they opened the inn. She's been living with Crohn's disease for the past four years. She recently started a new medication and is responding quite well." Joy smiled.

Nick's shoulders tensed. Hearing that this woman was living a normal and productive life with the disease sent a shock wave through his body.

"I think the boys will have a really good time," Joy said as she connected a piece of the puzzle.

Jordan lifted his head and crinkled his brow. "My mommy died from Cwones disease."

"It's Crohn's," Tyler corrected his brother. "He has trouble with words that have an *r* in them. He's getting better, though. He did speech therapy in Chicago," Tyler said before directing his attention back to the puzzle.

Joy fixed her eyes on Nick, but he looked away. He didn't want to see pity—the typical look he got from people when they heard about his wife. Following her death, going to work each day had been torture. The words of comfort and encouragement he'd received from his coworkers did nothing to ease his guilt. He knew they meant well, but if they'd known the truth, they would have been giving him a look of disgrace. In the end, he'd taken a leave of absence to try to deal with his grief.

Bella broke the silence that lingered. "So, will you come to the resort? It will be so much fun."

The boys looked up, their eyes hungry for a yes from their father. How could he say no? The twins deserved to have fun even if the idea of attending the event turned his stomach into a giant knot. "Well, if it's mandatory, I can't exactly leave the two of you home alone... I've seen that movie." He forced a smile.

Giggles filled the room.

Nick swallowed hard as he searched for a reason not to take Jordan and Tyler. The truth was, there were a million reasons, but the biggest one tore pieces of his heart every day. How could he attend an event for Crohn's that would support others, when he hadn't even helped his own wife?

Friday morning, the school cafeteria was a beehive of activity with adults getting their caffeine fix from the various lattes being served at the coffee bar and children loaded up with sugary sweets.

Nick had learned the annual bake sale was another way the school earned money so teachers didn't have to assume the cost of supplies for their classrooms. Glancing around the room, he decided whoever had this idea was a genius.

"Did you try one of your peanut butter chocolate chip cookies?" Joy asked as she approached holding treats wrapped in a napkin. She wore a pair of fitted jeans and a bright red sweatshirt with the school's logo. Casual Friday was another idea Nick liked about the school.

Even dressed casually, Joy looked beautiful. His

breath hitched before speaking. "Actually, I was a little afraid to try. After we went home last night I kept thinking I might have forgotten to mix in that second cup of sugar."

Joy laughed. "Oh, no, you got it in there. These are delicious and so gooey, especially if you zap them for a few seconds in the microwave." She took another bite, leaving a smudge of chocolate on her upper lip. "They're just the way I love them."

She looked adorable and the happiest he'd seen her since he'd returned to the valley. Maybe she was getting used to having him around again, or maybe that was wishful thinking and she'd just had too much sugar this morning.

"I wanted to thank you and Bella again for having me and the boys over last night. If it weren't for you, we would have been up until the wee hours of the morning baking and probably setting off the smoke detector. Tyler and Jordan had a great time." He paused and held her gaze. "I enjoyed it, too."

Joy tucked a loose strand of hair behind her ear and smiled. "It was fun. The children seemed to get along really well."

"I think we did, too." He threw a quick wink in her direction. "Seriously, though, it was kind of you to help me out. Since we moved, I feel as though I'm still struggling to get us settled, so you really came to our rescue."

"That's what neighbors do here—help each other. Small-town living isn't for everyone, but I can't imagine being anywhere else." She gazed around the cafeteria.

"Speaking of helping out, Jordan is so excited for his lesson tonight. As soon as he woke up, he started talking nonstop about it."

A smile parted Joy's lips. "Funny, it was the first thing I thought about when I woke up this morning, too. I'm really looking forward to it myself."

Nick's heart was full. Being back in his childhood community, surrounded by people who really cared about one another, was beginning to make him feel whole again. Moving was definitely one of the best decisions he'd made in a long time. If he were being honest with himself and with Joy, he was actually as excited about tonight as Jordan.

Chapter Five

Later that evening, Joy glanced at the quartz clock hanging on her bathroom wall—six forty-five. Fifteen minutes—that was all the time she had to make herself presentable. Judging by her reflection in the mirror, she'd need more like one hour and fifteen minutes. This morning at the bake sale, after speaking with Nick, her excitement about giving Jordan his first lesson had ramped up a couple of notches. She couldn't deny the fact that spending the evening with the Capello men was a nice change from her typical Friday night—home alone with a bowl of popcorn and a Hallmark movie. After school, she'd stopped by to visit Faith, who'd been thrilled to hear about her sister's plans this evening. At six thirty, Joy had found herself racing through the front door like a wild woman and running late.

She reached for her comb and raked it through her tangled hair. Outside, the northwest winds were howling, so she opted to go with a loose ponytail. During the bake sale, the twins had begged her to come over for Chinese food before the piano lesson. She doubted Nick was too keen on the idea, but he had suggested she arrive at seven o'clock. She'd only agreed for Jordan's sake. He seemed so happy about the lessons. After learning of their mother's death, Joy felt a need to protect the twins. Jordan seemed extra sensitive, though. He was a special child who was beginning to occupy more space in her heart, which wasn't a good thing, given he was Nick's son.

Fifteen minutes later, dressed in black jeans and a yellow turtleneck sweater, Joy pulled on her coat and headed across the street. Never in her wildest dreams had she thought Nick Capello would be living a stone's throw from her own house.

As she climbed the front porch steps of the quaint Cape Cod home, she paused when she heard laughter and voices coming from the other side of the door…the sounds of a happy family enjoying time together. Her heart squeezed when she realized anyone standing outside of her front door would only hear silence. No family resided within her walls. She'd come to terms with the fact that this was something that would never change, but still, swells of doubt and fear carried the reminder of what could have been.

Her gentle knock ignited a firestorm of cheers and the squeaking of tennis shoes across the hardwood floor. When the door whipped open, Jordan and Tyler stood grinning from ear to ear.

"Miss Kellihuh!" Jordan lunged toward Joy and wrapped his arms around her waist. Her knees went weak and she wished he'd never let go.

"We've been waiting for you. We wanted to show you our room," Tyler said as he reached for her hand and pulled her inside.

"You've got quite the fan club living under this roof."

Nick stood across the foyer wearing a casual smile and a crisp white shirt that drew her attention to his broad shoulders.

Joy felt her cheeks warm before quickly turning her attention back to the boys. "Is everything all unpacked?"

"Come see!" the boys sang out as Maverick jumped and took quick licks on her hand.

She scanned the inside of the cozy space. They had just moved in. How could there be so much warmth and love already inside of this home? She had lived in her house for years and it was like a hollow shell. It was only a roof over her head—no family memories were being created.

Jordan and Tyler pulled Joy down the hallway. Her eyes popped when she stepped inside of the twins' room. Candid framed photographs of the boys covered the walls. She turned to Nick. "Did you take all of these photos?"

He nodded. "I took up photography about a year ago."

Tyler stepped toward Joy. "Our mommy used to take all of the pictures—but she can't anymore."

Silence hung in the air as Joy glanced at Nick. His face flushed as he raked his hand through his hair.

Joy strolled around the room, appreciating each shot. "These really look like they were done by a professional." She stopped in front of the photo of the boys and a strikingly beautiful young woman. With golden blond hair that skimmed her shoulders, her smile lit up her pale blue eyes. The photo had to have been taken before she got ill. Joy's stomach twisted when she realized it was their mother. The three were sitting in a pile of vibrant, colorful autumn leaves. Jordan and Tyler were laughing as they both looked up at their mom. The picture radiated love—they adored her…and now she was gone.

She decided not to comment on that photo, but instead moved on and laughed at the picture of the boys covered in paint with their mother standing nearby with her hands on her hips. Her body language indicated she was upset by the mess, but her smile told a different story. "You two look like you were having fun."

Jordan stepped toward the photograph and placed his tiny hand on the frame. "That was the last pictuwe of me and Tyler with our mommy." His lower lip quivered.

A hush blanketed the room as the four stood staring at the wall. The sound of the doorbell chiming broke the silence.

"There's the food. Let's go eat—I'm starving." Nick spoke in an upbeat tone, an obvious attempt to lighten the mood.

Tyler tore from the room and his father followed behind. Joy glanced down at Jordan, whose eyes remained fixated on his mother. "Are you hungry, sweetie?"

Jordan nodded and placed his hand in hers. At that moment, a pebble from the wall Joy had built around her heart broke free.

An hour later with only one egg roll remaining on the plate, Joy pushed herself away from the table and began to clear the dishes.

Nick sprang to his feet. "Not so fast. We don't allow our guests to do manual labor in this house."

Joy laughed and carried the dishes to the kitchen sink. "It's the least I can do after you graciously invited me for dinner." The past hour had been like her dreams on most nights—laughing and sharing stories at the dinner table with her family. Of course, she needed no reminder that real life was never like her dreams. She'd come to accept it, but it didn't make it any less painful.

"Is it time for our lesson, Miss Kellihuh?" Jordan came to the sink carrying his plate.

She looked down and smiled. "That's nice of you to help me." Joy took the dish and ran it under the warm water. "We can start the lesson as soon as I finish up here."

"Nonsense. Tyler and I will take care of these. You two go get started." Nick stepped beside Joy and turned off the faucet. His spicy cologne teased her nose.

"I'll go get my music book," Jordan announced as he raced from the kitchen. Tyler trailed behind in a probable attempt to avoid helping with the dishes.

Nick turned to Joy. "I'm surprised he ate any dinner. He's been so excited about this lesson."

"I've been excited, too. He's such a compassionate little boy," Joy said as she reached inside of her tote bag sitting on the counter and pulled out some of her own sheet music.

"He's always been more sensitive than Tyler."

"Can I ask you something, Nick?" Joy hesitated for a moment, not wanting to overstep her boundaries, but she had to know.

"Of course."

"After your wife passed away, did the boys receive any counseling to help them understand what was happening?" Joy noticed Nick's jaw tighten. "I'm sorry. It's none of my business… Forget I asked."

Nick nodded as he loaded the dishes into the dishwasher. "It's okay. Yes, they did. According to the school counselor, Tyler did better than Jordan."

Joy wasn't surprised by that statement. "How so?"

"She said he wouldn't talk. Anything she asked him, he just sat there staring at the ground."

Joy's heart squeezed. She knew the pain of losing a parent, but she'd been so young when her parents were killed in a car crash. She only remembered snippets about them, like pieces of edited film, scattered on the floor. "Do you think maybe he senses that you're uncomfortable discussing his mother?" The hum of the refrigerator filled the silence.

"Jordan is waiting for you," he croaked.

Her stomach squeezed. "I'm sorry, Nick." She turned on her heel and headed into the living room. It was no wonder Jordan seemed open to talking about his mother with her. He obviously felt he couldn't talk to his father. Perhaps Jordan thought it would make his daddy too sad. Whatever the case, she couldn't help but wonder if there was something else Nick was refusing to bring up.

A half an hour into the lesson, Joy realized Jordan's skills were much more advanced than she had expected. "You're really very good. I think maybe you could give *me* lessons."

Jordan giggled and squirmed on the oak bench. "Thank you, but you're pwobably ten times better than me. But I'm going to keep pwacticing, even if Tyler thinks it's silly."

"I'm happy to hear you say that. It's important not to let others steal your joy. I hope you'll remember that." Of course, each day she needed to remind herself, but it was a constant battle.

"I will—I pwomise." He turned to Joy and looked up. "Miss Kellihuh, how come you don't have any kids? You'd be a weally good mommy."

Joy knew he didn't mean any harm with his innocent

question, but his words were like daggers shredding her heart into pieces. "It wasn't in God's plans, sweetheart."

"Was it God's plan to take my mommy away fwom me?" He bit his lower lip. "Why would He do something so mean?"

Joy was the last person to explain why God allowed terrible things to happen to good people. Of course, in her case, maybe He didn't think she was good. She had made the choice to get in the car with Scotty. But Jordan wasn't talking about her. He was referring to his mother. "Oh, sweetheart, God wasn't trying to be mean to you. I know it's hard to understand, but bad things do happen in this world. We have to trust that God knows what He's doing and somehow He will bring some good from the situation." By the expression on Jordan's face, he was as confused as she was.

"But I pwayed—a lot. She was always in the bath-woom and she kept getting skinnior. I asked God to make huh bettuh…but He didn't listen."

"Jordan!"

Maverick barked as Nick's voice echoed from the foyer. He'd been listening.

"It's okay… We were just talking," Joy explained as she took notice of the pain in Nick's eyes while Jordan quivered against her arm.

"I think it's time to say good-night," Nick said.

"But, Daddy, what about my lesson? You pwomised me."

Nick rubbed the back of his neck. "It's getting late." He obviously wanted her to leave.

Joy stood. "We'll finish up another day, sweetie. Don't you worry." She glanced at her watch. "I'm a little tired, anyway."

Twenty minutes later, following a quick shower, Joy settled into her favorite comfy chair, in the corner of her bedroom. As she sipped her cup of chamomile tea, she wondered how an evening that had begun with laughter and good food had come to an abrupt end. The expression on Jordan's face when she'd exited the house left her heartbroken. No words were uttered by Nick… not even a good-night. With his arms folded across his chest and his face expressionless, she couldn't help but think maybe she'd been wrong about the happy family living behind the walls of the Capello house.

Tuesday afternoon Nick inhaled a deep breath before entering the school's auditorium. Since Friday night, he'd done his best to avoid running into Joy. More like hide from her. Saturday morning, while out on his front porch watering his pots of pansies that seemed to thrive in the winter sunlight, he'd spotted her car cruising down the street. He'd slipped inside and watched from the window as she'd pulled into her driveway and begun to unload her groceries.

There'd been a part of him that had longed to go over and help her as she made multiple trips in and out of her house. But he hadn't been quite ready to face her again and risk having to explain his behavior. He couldn't blame her for practically running out of his house after he'd snapped when he'd heard the conversation she'd been having with Jordan. It wasn't her fault. She'd been doing what was in her nature…listening. Poor Jordan had spent the rest of the evening in his room in tears, while Nick had tried to prepare for his upcoming interview, to no avail. He knew he'd been wrong to react like he had. Hearing his son talk about his sick mother had washed in another wave of guilt. It had broken his heart to see Jordan so sad, but especially his questioning of God's will.

"Daddy!" Tyler ran down the aisle with his arms flailing.

Nick's stomach twisted when he saw the look of fear in his son's eyes. "What is it, Tyler—what's wrong?"

"It's Jordan… He said he doesn't want to be in the play."

That couldn't be. Just the other day, he'd seemed so excited. Unlike his brother, he didn't want a leading role. But he'd seemed thrilled to be cast as a mushroom, especially when he found out Mrs. Buser planned to make his costume. She was the best seamstress in town.

Nick scanned the stage and spied Jordan sitting alone on a folding chair. "I'll go see what's up. Don't worry, bud." With a deep breath, he scaled the steps leading to the stage and crossed the polished wood floors. "Jordan, you okay, buddy?"

He nodded and wiped his cheek.

A ripple of guilt seeped over Nick as he noticed the same sad look in Jordan's eyes that he'd seen the other night. Protecting his sons from pain and heartbreak had become his number one priority since their mother had passed away. But why hadn't it been before? Why hadn't he protected their mother and sought out proper treatment for her? He'd been too self-absorbed. His stomach tightened as he squatted down in front of his son. "Jordan, talk to me, please." He brushed his son's hair away from his eyes. "Tyler said you don't want to be in the play. I thought you were excited about it?" Just last night, he'd overheard the boys giggling in their room as Tyler practiced his lines.

"I was, but I'm not anymow." He sighed.

Nick turned at the sound of footsteps approaching from behind.

"Is everything okay over here?" Joy asked in a whispered tone.

"Apparently, this little guy no longer wants to be in the play." Nick regarded Joy with a questioning eye.

Joy reached out and tucked the pad of her thumb under the child's chin. "You don't? Why not, sweetie?"

Jordan sniffled before answering. "Some of the kids wuh teasing me," he stuttered.

Nick's jaw tightened. "About being a mushroom?" When it came to teasing, kids could be so cruel. While teaching in Chicago, each year Nick taught a lesson plan on bullying. It was something he'd never tolerate in or outside of the classroom.

Jordan only shook his head.

Joy took a seat in the empty chair. "You can tell us, sweetheart. Were they teasing you about the way you talk?"

"Yeah." He sniffed twice.

Nick looked over at Joy. She was good. How did she know that was what had his son so upset?

"They laughed at me when I told them I was going to be a mushwoom." He rubbed his eyes. "One kid said since I talk funny I could only play a twee or a mushwoom. Is that why I don't have any lines to memowize, like Tyler does?"

Joy ran her hand down his cheek. "Of course not. You were excited to play the part."

"Not anymow—do I have to?" His eyes pleaded for a no.

Nick wasn't thrilled to see his son back down to the

bullies, but he didn't want him to be unhappy either. He glanced at Joy, who gave him a slight nod. "No, if you don't want to play the mushroom, we'll cast some-one else in the role. Are you sure this is what you want to do, son?"

Jordan sat in silence.

"I have an idea," Joy broke in. "Why don't you play the overture?"

Jordan's brow crinkled. "I'm not sure I know how to play that. Is it a puhson?"

Nick and Joy shared a smile.

"No, sweetie. An overture is the music that's played before the start of a movie or, in our case, a play," Joy explained in a caring tone.

His eyes popped. "You mean…play the piano in fwont of the whole school?"

Nick couldn't imagine Jordan would agree to Joy's suggestion. For one, he was way too shy, and plus, he never wanted anyone outside of the family to know he played.

"Yes, but we could situate the piano on the stage in a way that you wouldn't even have to see the audience. I could sit beside you and we could pretend you're play-ing for me in your living room." She winked. "What do you say? You play so beautifully, Jordan. You shouldn't be embarrassed by your talent."

Nick kept a close eye on his son as his brow furrowed while contemplating Joy's suggestion. Playing in front of the entire school would be a huge step for Jordan. He never enjoyed being the center of attention, but perhaps this would help him to overcome his shyness.

Jordan looked up at Joy. "Do you pwomise you'll sit beside me the whole time?"

She reached for his hand and gave it two squeezes. "Yes. I'll never leave your side."

"I can't wait to tell Ty that I'm back in the play!" Jordan sprang out of his chair and ran across the stage toward his brother.

Nick's heart was full. "You were amazing."

Joy's cheeks flushed. "What?"

"With Jordan—I could never talk him into performing on stage."

She pushed her hair away from her face. "I'm sure you could. He just needed a little nudge."

"He trusts you…probably more than me," Nick admitted. "You're great with the kids, Joy." He bit down on his lower lip. Maybe she did deserve to be principal. It was true, she didn't have her master's yet, but she had a way with children that could never be taught from a book. Had he been wrong thinking he was the man for the job?

Chapter Six

Saturday morning, Joy laced up her running shoes and pulled her hair into a high and tight ponytail. Being a creature of habit, she ran five miles several mornings a week. She always headed out at 6:00 a.m. rain or shine, except on Sunday, when she typically ran in the evening. Of course, when the heavy mountain snows hit, she was forced to use her treadmill. Thankfully, so far this winter the roads had remained clear.

Outside, her feet pounded a steady rhythm against the pavement. She loved the feel of the mountain air pulsating through her lungs. Inhaling a deep breath of the frigid air was a reminder to those living in Whispering Slopes that Old Man Winter had taken his grip. They were due for a big snow. Although each season provided its own beauty, spring had always been her favorite.

As she continued her way down the winding country road, her thoughts turned to what had transpired before rehearsal earlier in the week. She was thankful she'd been able to convince Jordan to remain a participant in the play. Playing the overture would be a first step to getting him to come out of his shell. He was such a sweet boy with a loving heart.

They'd had another rehearsal on Thursday where she'd insisted on working with Bella in her role as Little Red Riding Hood. If possible, she had to avoid helping Tyler with his part. She didn't want to hurt his feelings, but she needed to protect her own. Staying as far away from the Big Bad Wolf was the only way to keep the horrible memories from bubbling to the surface.

An hour later, after a quick shower and a toasted onion bagel, Joy snatched her car keys and headed out the door. She'd promised Faith and Joshua she'd come over to the resort a little earlier to keep Bella entertained while they got things ready for the school's winter festival.

A few minutes later, she approached the entrance to the Black Bear Resort. Hitting the turn signal, she began the slow climb up the steep, Fraser fir–lined driveway. At the top, the parking lot was getting full. She circled to the back row and found an empty space next to Mrs. Buser's delivery van.

Placing the vehicle in Park, she grabbed the last few sips of her coffee and headed inside.

"Aunt Joy!" Bella greeted her in the foyer.

They exchanged a hug and Joy kissed her warm, pink cheek.

Joy still couldn't get over the inn's transformation. When Joshua and Faith were deeded the property by his father, Joshua had made Faith a promise. Being a man of his word, he'd expanded the Black Bear Inn into a massive resort and restored the old family home where she and Faith had grown up with their grandparents. Later, their grandfather had financial difficulties and the land had been purchased by Joshua's father. He'd done a fabulous job with all of the renovations of the home, including many modern upgrades.

Joy looked down at Bella, dressed in blue jeans with tiny embroidered daisies on the back pockets. Her heart melted. Bella's brown-sugar curls were pulled back into a loose ponytail. "Are you excited for today?"

Bella grabbed her hand and led Joy toward the kitchen. "Yes! I can't wait for Tyler and Jordan to get here. We're going to have so much fun."

Joy knew the boys would have a good time. She hoped Nick would as well. He hadn't seemed the same since the night of Jordan's first lesson. Had listening to his son talk about missing his mother triggered too many painful memories? If anyone knew about triggers, she did, especially with the play and having the wolf lurking in the shadows…just waiting to pounce.

Early morning sunlight filtered through the kitchen window, casting a golden light on Faith's fair complexion as she rinsed the breakfast dishes.

Coffee. She needed gallons of the stuff to get through this day. She'd been up late last night studying for another online exam she planned to take next week. Thankfully, because the degree program was self-paced, it allowed for flexibility. Of course, since Nick had returned, Joy felt pressured to step up her speed. The sooner she could get that piece of paper, the better.

"Good morning, sis." She released Bella's hand and headed toward the coffee maker for a refill. Bella whizzed out of the room.

Faith dried her hands. "Hey—thanks for coming so early. I feel like there's a million things left to do." She glanced at her watch. "It's already after eight o'clock. A couple of the events start at ten."

Joy refilled her cup with the steaming brew and took a quick sip. "Relax—there's plenty of time. Besides, the school staff should start to trickle in anytime now. They'll be eager to help, especially if we get them loaded up on caffeine."

For the next fifteen minutes the two sisters chatted. Joy updated her on Nick's wife and what had transpired during the last few rehearsals.

The sound of whistling put an end to the conversation.

"Mommy, what time will Tyler and Jordan be here?"

Joy and Faith exchanged a glance.

"I don't know, sweetie, but even if they don't come, your entire school will be here. You'll have plenty of other children to play with," her mother responded as she twirled Bella's ponytail.

"Yeah, but it won't be as much fun." She turned on her heel and then spun around. "Oh, yeah, Daddy wanted me to tell you there aren't any hamburger buns," Bella announced as she skipped out of the room.

Faith sprang from her chair and grabbed her phone. She sent a quick text to Joshua, who was out on the slopes with some of his crew. Her arms dropped to her side when her phone chimed a response.

"What's wrong?"

"We've got over two hundred patties and no buns. Joshua thought I was getting them and I thought he was."

The perfect opportunity to take a break from talking about Nick. Joy grabbed her coffee mug and pushed away from the table. "No worries. I'll go to the store." She turned on the faucet and rinsed her cup.

"You're a lifesaver, sweetie. Mr. Swanson is holding

the order at the market." Faith scurried to the pantry and removed her purse. "Here, take this." She whipped out a credit card and handed it to her sister.

"You got it. I'll be back in less than a half an hour and then you can put me to work." Joy grabbed her bag and flung the strap over her shoulder. "See you in a bit."

Outside in the parking lot, she walked at a fast pace toward her car. Funny, although it was parked on a flat surface, the passenger side appeared lower. Joy walked to the other side of the vehicle. Oh, great. The rear tire was as flat as a sand dollar and she had no spare. Not that she'd know how to change it if she did. She'd kept meaning to have Joshua show her how it was done, but it had always slipped her mind.

She turned at the sound of tires crunching on the gravel lot. The familiar silver SUV with Nick behind the wheel caused her pulse to quicken.

He pulled his vehicle beside her disabled car and rolled down the window. "Need some help, Jo Jo?"

Her heart twisted at the sound of her old nickname. It seemed like a lifetime ago since she'd heard it. As kids, Nick had come up with the name, and to this day, he was the only one who'd ever called her that.

The twins jumped out the moment they came to a stop. "Hi, Miss Kelliher! Can we go inside and see Bella?" Tyler begged.

"Hello, boys." Joy looked at Nick as he stepped out from his car, then turned her attention toward the twins. "Ah…if it's okay with your father."

"Can we? Can we?" Tyler and Jordan jumped up and down in circles.

"Are you sure it'll be okay with Faith?" Nick asked.

"Of course—anything to keep Bella occupied. It's been a busy morning for Faith and Joshua."

"Go ahead, but behave yourselves." Nick smiled at Joy. "They've been so excited. Ever since they got out of bed this morning, they've talked nonstop about seeing her today."

Joy smiled. "She's a special little girl."

"Yes, she is. Do you want to pop your lock? I'll put your spare on for you."

Her cheeks warmed as she looked at the ground and kicked a rock. She'd been grateful that since the last rehearsal, they'd had a little more peace between them. As long as they didn't discuss the principal position or his ex-wife, things seemed to stay civil.

"Let me guess—no spare?"

She shrugged. "What can I say? I was never a Girl Scout."

"Okay, then. Can I give you a lift somewhere?"

A quick glance at her watch told her things would really start to get busy soon. "I don't want to trouble you. I'll just borrow Faith's car."

"That's not necessary. Please, let me help out. That's what I'm here for. Besides, it's the least I could do after you were so good to Jordan, suggesting he play the overture. You're pretty incredible with him."

She fingered the gold chain around her neck. Faith didn't have time to run the errand and Joy didn't have time to deal with the butterflies that were flitting in her stomach since Nick had arrived. "Okay, I just need to go to the grocery store. There's been a hamburger bun emergency."

He chuckled. "Sounds serious."

The tension released in her neck. "I guess that sounds

strange, but it's the truth. We need two hundred rolls, pronto. People around here like their burgers."

"Well, let's go, then. But first, let me run inside to let the boys know and make sure it's okay with Faith to leave them here to play with Bella," he said.

Minutes later, Joy secured her seat belt and slid her cell phone from her purse. "Excuse me a second. I need to call the auto club."

Following a short drive, they pulled into the parking lot at the market. She'd been relieved to have been put on hold for so long when she called for assistance—no unnecessary small talk had been required, so she was guaranteed not to say the wrong thing to Nick.

Once inside the store, Joy hurried to customer service to pay.

"Go ahead and pull your car around front. We'll get you loaded up and on your way in a jiffy." Mr. Swanson smiled and handed Joy the receipt.

"Thank you so much for your help," Joy said as she and Nick exited the store.

The sun beamed into her eyes when they stepped out of the store. She reached into her purse for her sunglasses and slid them on.

They climbed into the car and buckled up. Nick put the SUV in Drive and eased up to the front of the store. An uncomfortable silence hung inside of the vehicle as Joy twisted her purse strap around her finger and then unraveled it.

"Nick, I wanted to apologize again for questioning you about getting help for the boys and for yourself. Sometimes I don't know when to mind my own business. It's just…"

"What is it, Joy?"

"Jordan tugged on my heartstrings the night of his piano lesson. He's so confused about his mother and God's plan. He had so many questions about his mother, but I didn't have answers for him. I guess I got upset that you didn't step up to the plate and ease his troubled mind."

A slight shake of his head told her she'd once again overstepped her bounds.

"Here I go again—I'm sorry. I'm just overprotective when it comes to children," Joy said as her shoulders relaxed when she spotted Mr. Swanson approaching the vehicle with the flatbed loaded with the buns. Somehow, she'd have to keep her feelings under control if she was going to make it through this day.

The resort was a beehive of activity when Joy and Nick pulled into the parking lot. Groups of skiers milled about, anxious to hit the slopes covered with several inches of artificial snow. When the twins spotted their father and Joy unloading the buns, they raced to the car. Bella followed behind.

"Daddy! You should have seen it." Tyler stopped to catch his breath. "Miss Faith took us sledding! We were flying down the hill really fast. It was the most fun ever!" His face beamed.

Nick's chest lightened. He was happy to see the boys having such a good time. He'd been nervous about uprooting the boys and moving them to a strange town, but seeing the joy in their faces today, he knew he'd made the right decision.

"So what do you guys want to do next?" He scanned the children's jubilant expressions and then locked his gaze on Joy.

A Mother for His Twins

Tyler spoke up first. "Can we go on the hot air balloon ride, Daddy? That would be so cool."

Jordan remained quiet.

"I'm not sure if that's such a good idea, guys." He hated to put a damper on the day, but with Jordan's fear of heights, Nick didn't want him to go along with the group and end up being scared in the balloon.

"Aw…come on," Tyler and Bella whined in unison.

"Herb's been taking people up in his balloon for years, Nick. The boys will be safe," Joy said as she looked up into the sky. "Besides, the weather is ideal. The winds are calm and the temperature feels nice."

Bella and Tyler ran around in circles, while Jordan took a step back. Nick leaned toward Joy, away from the children, and rubbed the back of his neck. "I'm sure it's safe. I'm just a little worried about Jordan."

Concern spread across her face. "What's wrong? He's not sick, is he?"

"No, he's afraid of heights. Of course, he's not going to admit that in front of Bella. He's not as fearless as Tyler. He wasn't always like that, but after his mother died he seemed to become more fearful."

Joy turned to the children before responding. "I think it might be good for him. We can all go up together—trust me, it'll be fine. I think he'll love it!"

Nick stepped a little closer to her, catching a whiff of her fragrance and feeling a little dizzy. It reminded him of the summertime honeysuckle in full bloom. He and Joy used to explore the fields in search of the vines. "Are you sure about this?"

She smiled. "Absolutely, just—let me go and double-check with Faith that it's okay for Bella to go."

He watched as Joy ran off to find her sister. She

looked like that young girl he'd fallen in love with a lifetime ago. Was this a good idea? All of them going up into the balloon together...like a family? It was one thing for Joy to be the boys' teacher, but spending time together outside of the classroom, the twins, especially Jordan, were obviously becoming more attached to her. But as he watched Tyler bursting with excitement, how could he disappoint them by saying no to their first hot air balloon ride?

A short time later sunshine penetrated through the mountaintops as the balloon drifted across the painted blue sky. Nick felt as though he could reach up and touch one of the white puffs of clouds that drifted overhead. His thoughts turned to Joy and all of the things he wanted to tell her. There was so much he wished had turned out differently. For now, the regrets of the past seemed to glide away, but he knew that once he was back on the ground, the real world would be waiting for him. But for now, he'd enjoy this glorious day.

"Look, Daddy! Our car looks like a tiny bug." Tyler pointed down toward the parking lot as his father held him.

Nick kept an eye on Jordan, who huddled close to Joy with his eyes squeezed shut. He rested his hand on his son's shoulder. "You okay, buddy?"

Without looking, Jordan nodded.

"Jor, look! You're going to miss everything." Tyler wiggled from Nick's grasp and tugged on his brother's arm, but Jordan only snuggled closer against Joy's waist, shaking his head.

"He's a scaredy-cat."

"I am not!" Jordan shouted as he lurched forward then quickly stepped back.

Nick felt for his son. "Tyler, it's not right to tease your brother because he has a fear of heights. Everyone is afraid of something."

Jordan looked up at his dad with hopeful eyes. "Except you, wight?"

"I'm afraid of fire," Bella chimed in. "My daddy was a firefighter and he died fighting a fire." Her smile faded as she looked down.

Jordan pulled away from Joy and gingerly tiptoed toward Bella. "I'm sowwy about youw daddy, Bella."

"Me, too," Tyler said as he looked at his brother. "I'm sorry I teased you, Jor."

Nick watched with a knowing grin. They might fight like cats and dogs sometimes, but they really loved each other. And now it appeared they'd adopted a sister.

Jordan stepped closer to the edge of the basket. "Daddy, can you pick me up so I can see ovuh?" He took a peek and smiled. "This isn't as scawy as I thought it would be."

For the next twenty minutes, the balloon circled Whispering Slopes. Nick was finally home. He prayed to himself, thanking God for the beautiful day, his healthy children and this special time with Joy. Since they'd boarded the balloon, he and Joy seemed to have forgotten about the past and what the future might hold with the principal position. Once their feet hit the ground, it would be back to reality. Then he'd have to keep his head out of the clouds and his focus on his goal.

With the excitement of the hot air balloon ride behind them, the children were ready to move on to more stimulation.

"Let's go for a pony ride," Bella suggested as she skipped along the trampled path. Her hair escaped the loose ponytail and flopped into her eyes.

Tyler pulled on his father's arm. "I want to go sledding again."

"But we already did that. You'll love the ponies, Ty," Bella exclaimed.

Nick couldn't be any happier. It had been a long time since he'd seen his boys so excited and carefree.

Joy glanced down at Bella. "First, we need to check in with your mommy." When Joy's phone chimed, she pulled it from her coat pocket and answered the call. "Okay, I'll be right there," she said into the device.

Slipping the phone back into the pocket, she turned to the group. "That was the auto club. They're here to fix the tire. Let me take care of them and then we'll let your mommy know your feet are back on the ground."

Bella giggled. "Okay, but will you promise we can see the horses after?"

Joy reached for her niece's hand and gave it a squeeze. "I promise."

Twenty minutes later, the group trekked down the shaded tree-lined path that led to the stables. A thin layer of snow crunched underneath their shoes.

"Why is there snow here, Miss Kellihuh?" Jordan asked as he stopped to try to gather a handful.

"We had a couple of inches of snow right before you came to Whispering Slopes. Since it's shady through here, it hasn't melted."

"I wish we'd have a blizzard," Tyler said as he kicked the icy crystals.

Joy smiled. "Don't worry—we'll get our share of snow."

When they reached the end of the trail, Nick's lips parted. "This is incredible." The wide-open pasture with gentle rolling land was surrounded by a snowcapped mountain range.

"You certainly don't see this kind of beauty in Chicago. I've missed this."

A slight aroma of manure wafted in the air as they approached the stables. Children's laughter echoed from the paddock.

"Look—there's the ponies!" Tyler shouted as the children took off toward the cedar structure.

"Daddy, I want to ride the black one," Tyler announced.

Leaning against the fence, Nick noticed Jordan watching the pony that appeared to be missing his tail. With the exception of a big white circle on its nose, its color was solid chestnut.

"How about you, buddy?" Nick glanced down at Jordan. "Which one do you want to ride?"

He watched as his son continued to study the tailless pony.

"I think I want that one." He pointed.

Joy looked at Nick and smiled. He knew that although she'd only known the boys for a short period of time, she truly understood and appreciated Jordan's sensitive side.

"Why that one?" Nick asked, although he was pretty sure of the reason.

Jordan looked up at his father. He squinted when the sun hit his eyes. "Well, you might not have noticed, but he doesn't have a tail. He might not get picked too much because people think he's diffewent."

Nick beamed with pride. "And you don't think that?"

Jordan turned his gaze back on the pony. "Oh, no, I think that's what makes him special."

Joy winked at Nick, causing his pulse to quicken.

He bent down and raised his son into his arms. "You know what? I think you're pretty special, too."

Fifteen minutes later, the children were saddled up

and being led around the ring by the volunteers. The kids were all giggles and smiles.

Nick and Joy had settled in at a nearby picnic table, enjoying the mountain range. Despite temperatures in the forties, the bright sunlight provided warmth. He inhaled a deep, cleansing breath. He'd missed the invigorating air the years he'd lived in Chicago. Sadly, he'd smelled more smog than good clean air in the city.

Since the ride in the balloon, Nick couldn't seem to peel his eyes away from Joy. The sunlight was touching the side of her cheek, highlighting her porcelain complexion. He willed his heart to slow. She was even more beautiful than he'd remembered, but there again was that unexplained sadness in her eyes as she appeared unable to look away from the children.

Finally, she turned to him. "They're special boys, Nick. You've done a really good job with them."

Some days he felt as though he wasn't doing anything right when it came to raising his sons. Even on the easiest days, trying to be both father and mother was difficult. Still, he knew he owed it to his wife to raise the boys with a love for God and strong values so they'd grow up to be good husbands—unlike he'd been.

"Thank you. That means a lot, Joy."

She locked eyes with his and his heart hammered in his chest, exactly like it had so many years ago when she'd looked at him.

"You should be proud."

He did feel a sense of pride when it came to his sons, but not when he looked back on his past where women were concerned—well, Joy and Michelle. They'd been the only female relationships in his life. His marriage had been a road filled with regrets. Could he make up for any of those mistakes? Was this reunion with Joy God's way of giving him a second chance at love? Nonsense. He didn't deserve another opportunity. This thin mountain air was just messing with his brain.

Joy turned her attention back to the children as he squirmed on the bench. There were so many questions he wanted to ask her, but he wasn't sure if she was ready to talk. Not knowing when he might have the opportunity, he sucked in a breath and exhaled. "Can I ask you something?" He paused for her reaction, but there wasn't any. "You don't have to answer if you don't want to."

"You're making me a little nervous." She smiled. Her brown eyes with flecks of green sparkled when their gazes connected. "Go ahead."

"Well, it's obvious how much you love children, and you're so good with them." He swallowed the lump that clogged his throat. "My boys bring me so much pleasure. They're the greatest joy in my life…the reason I get out of bed each day. I can't help but wonder if you want to have children of your own someday?"

Joy's shoulders straightened, and the smile she'd worn most of the day slipped from her lips, replaced by a far-off sadness. "I can't talk about this, Nick…especially with you." She started to get up from the table when her phone chimed. Slipping it from her pocket, she glanced at the screen. "It's a text from Faith. She wants to know if you can come and help Joshua carry some tables."

Nick stood. "Of course. Let's get the kids and head up to the house."

Joy looked over at the children as their ponies circled the paddock. They were all smiles and giggles. "Why don't you go? They're having a good time." She motioned her arm in their direction.

After his insensitive question to her about having children, she probably wanted a little time away from him. He couldn't blame her. "Okay, I'll be back as soon as I can," Nick said as he headed toward the path. She was right—he had no business asking her such a personal question. It was too soon. But there was a part of him that needed to know. There was so much about her that remained a mystery. He'd been gone so many years… Had she dated? Of course she had. She was a beautiful and loving woman. She'd probably had many dates. Had any turned serious? He wanted to know more about the time he'd been away, but what was the point? They were both vying for the same job and soon they'd be facing the biggest interview of their careers. When all was said and done, one would win and the other would lose. He couldn't imagine a friendship surviving those circumstances.

Chapter Seven

During the next twenty-five minutes Joy sat at the picnic table near the paddock in order to keep a close eye on the children as they circled the ring. Her hands shook as Nick's question filtered through her mind. Had it been what he'd asked her or thoughts of children with him that ignited this curt reaction to him? Over the years, he'd crept into her dreams. Sometimes they were still back in high school, but often they'd been happily married for years. When she dreamed they were married, it was always the same. They had two boys, a girl and a golden retriever named Chance.

With a kick to his pony, Tyler moved into a trot. The volunteer leading his horse had stepped away for a drink of water. Tyler's small shoulders bounced in stride. "Look, Miss Kelliher, no hands."

Joy looked in Tyler's direction. He straddled the pony with both hands up in the air. She jumped to her feet and raced to the fence. "Tyler, no! Hold on to the reins."

When the walnut-colored pony came to an abrupt stop, Tyler went flying.

"Ty!" Jordan cried out.

Joy yanked open the gate and sprinted toward the boy. He was sprawled on the ground holding his knee. He wasn't crying, so that had to be a good sign, wasn't it? But fear pooled in his eyes. She knelt next to him. "Where does it hurt, Tyler?" Guilt consumed her. It had been her responsibility to keep an eye on him. What if something was broken?

"I'm okay." Tyler looked up, squinting from the sun. "That's a short pony." He grinned.

"Are you sure you're not in any pain? You took a hard spill." She should have covered for the volunteer while she'd gone for a drink.

As all of the other volunteers gathered closer to make sure Tyler was okay, the guilt continued to fester. How could she tell Nick that his son was hurt because of her negligence? He'd trusted her.

"No, nothing hurts. I think I tore my jeans, though. I hope Daddy doesn't get upset… He doesn't like to sew patches."

"Tyler!" Nick's voice echoed through the pasture.

Joy turned and watched as Nick frantically sprinted toward his son, who remained splayed out on the ground.

"What happened? Are you hurt? Did the horse throw you?"

"I'm fine, Daddy. I was trying to show off. I've fallen off my bed before and it's higher than that pony. I'm okay. Can I ride some more?"

Nick lifted Tyler from the ground and threw a quick glance toward Joy. "No, I think you've had enough for one day."

Joy bit hard on her bottom lip as her stomach churned. "I'm so sorry, Nick. It was my fault. He would have never fallen if I'd been paying closer attention." Her eyes prickled with tears. "Tyler was my responsibility." She knew her mind had been preoccupied with Nick's earlier question. She was to blame. Tears pooled in her eyes.

Nick ran his hand along her shoulder. "Joy, it's okay. Really, little boys fall—it's what they do. Like Tyler said, he didn't have that far to fall. This wasn't your fault. Please, don't cry."

But it was. She was supposed to protect them just like she wanted to keep watch over all of her children at the school by becoming principal. Maybe Nick was right. Perhaps he was more qualified for the position. If she couldn't keep one innocent little boy safe, how could she ever maintain the safety of an entire school?

As the group meandered up the path toward the inn, a siren blared in the distance. Joy reached for Bella's hand, knowing the sound frightened her. The girl pulled loose and covered her ears. She hummed a song to drown out the noise.

Tyler looked over at his father. "What's she doing, Daddy?"

"Ty, shh…wemembuh, huh daddy," Jordan whispered.

As the siren grew louder, it became obvious the emergency vehicle was headed in their direction.

Bella wrapped her arms around Joy's waist. "Make it stop."

Joy's brow creased. "I can't, sweetie. Someone must need help, so the sound is a good thing. It means they'll be taken care of soon."

When the ambulance zipped into the entrance of the resort, Joy had a sinking feeling in her stomach. *Faith.* Something was wrong with her twin… She could feel it. She shot a look at Nick. "Keep the kids out here." She peeled herself away from Bella and sprinted toward the front door to the lobby.

A group of skiers stood congregated by the front desk, dressed in their neon ski suits and matching hats. They were ready to hit the slopes.

Joy raced into Faith's office. As she feared, her sister was on the floor. Two paramedics surrounded her as one placed an oxygen mask over her mouth.

"Joshua, what's happening?"

"She's unconscious." His face pale with panic did nothing to calm Joy's nerves. The walls closed in as the chatter of people circled the room. For a second, she forgot how to breathe.

"She was registering some of the skiers, and then she came in here to file some paperwork. She'd been fine earlier. I don't understand."

Joy hugged her brother-in-law tight as his eyes brimmed with tears. "She's tough." She expelled a deep breath. "Faith and the twins are going to be okay."

Things got a little too real for Joy when Faith was placed on the gurney. She rested her hand on the arm of one of the paramedics. "Is my sister going to be okay?"

The stocky dark-haired man turned to Joy. "At the moment her blood pressure is too high. We'll transport her to Valley Memorial. You can follow us." The two men whisked her twin out of the room, leaving Joy speechless.

She turned to Joshua. The look of fear on his face made her blood run cold. "You go on and ride with Faith. I'll get Bella and we'll meet you at the hospital. She'll be okay, so don't worry."

Bella… Her little niece had already experienced loss

when her father was killed. How would she react when she found out her mother had been taken to the hospital?

"Sweet Bella," Joshua cried out. "Please tell her that Mommy will be okay." He turned and sprinted out of the office. Joy followed.

Once outside, she scanned the property for Nick and the children. Blinded by the glaring sun, she hoped he'd kept the kids away from the ambulance, but they were nowhere in sight.

The ponies.

The children probably convinced Nick to take them back to the paddock.

Joy sprinted to the trail leading to the stables. *Please, God, let Faith and her twins be okay.* Her feet skidded on some icy mud, causing her to lose her footing.

Before she knew what was happening—*splat.* She hit the hard and cold ground. Her ankle twisted and was riddled with sharp shooting pains. Great. She tried to stand, but the pain seared to the bone. She dropped to her knees and reached for her phone in her back pocket. Staring at the screen, she couldn't think who to call. She didn't have Nick's number programmed into her phone and her sister was being transported to the hospital along with her crisis go-to guy, Joshua. Joy had no one. Her heart sank as she stuffed the phone into her jeans, forced to sit and wait for someone to come along. But who? She was stuck on a deserted trail. Alone. She should be used to it—being by herself—but after enjoying such a wonderful day, she felt even more lonesome.

Minutes later, the sounds of children's chatter echoed down the trail.

"Joy!"

Nick spotted her on the ground holding her ankle.

He sprinted toward her at top speed. "What happened? Are you okay?"

He dropped to his knees. "Is it broken?"

"I don't think so… I mean, I hope not. It really hurts, though." Joy watched Bella, dreading the thought of breaking the news to her about her mother.

"Can you put any weight on it?"

She shook her head. "I tried to stand up, but the pain is bad."

"Let's get that shoe off. We need to get you to the hospital for X-rays." He reached to pick her up.

"Wait!"

Nick jumped and pulled his hands away. "What is it? Did I hurt you?"

Joy looked at Bella and extended her hand. The child's face shrouded with fear. "Sweetie, I need to talk with you before we go."

Her niece took tiny steps toward her. "Are you going to be okay, Aunt Joy?"

She pulled Bella close and hugged her tight. "Yes, I'll be fine. I need to talk with you before we go to the hospital."

Bella's forehead crinkled.

"The siren you heard earlier—they came for your mommy, but she's going to be fine."

When her niece tried to break free, Joy held on a little tighter.

She sniffled. "But why did they take her?"

"They need to make sure the babies are safe."

"I want to see my mommy," Bella cried out.

Joy stroked her soft curls. "You will. We're going to the hospital now." She looked up. *Nick.* In the past he'd always been there for her, except for that night…but now he was here. He held her gaze.

"Can you give us a ride?"

Without answering, Nick scooped her up into his arms. Strong—just as she remembered. She shook away her thoughts. He was here to help her, nothing more. She needed to remember why he'd come back to Whispering Slopes. It wasn't for her. He was here for her job.

"Of course. I'll take you and Bella." He turned toward the twins. "Let's get going, boys. We need to hurry. Miss Kelliher needs to be examined by a doctor."

Disappointment and concern cloaked their faces. There wouldn't be any ice-skating or more pony rides. Not today.

As Nick worked his way up the path, she stole glimpses of the side of his clean-shaven face, and a sense of calm took hold. He still had those boyish good looks that she'd never forgotten. He smelled like a babbling creek on a warm spring day. She needed to make more of an effort to stop wondering where they would be today if his mother hadn't taken ill and his family hadn't left town.

Fifteen minutes later, Nick zipped his SUV in front of the emergency room.

Joy fidgeted in the passenger seat. Her ankle throbbed and was getting bigger by the minute.

Nick sprang from the vehicle and rounded to the other side. When he opened the door, he glanced at her bare foot. "I'm glad I had you take off your shoe. The ankle is swelling like an eggplant."

She put her arms around his neck as he lifted her from the seat. His leather jacket felt cool to the touch, and for a moment, she felt protected.

He raced through the door while the children ran along beside him.

"Is it okay to leave your car there?" Joy peered over her shoulder at his abandoned vehicle.

"It's fine for now. I need to get you into a wheelchair before I move it."

"What about my mommy? When can I see her?" Bella exclaimed.

Joy's heart sank. Of all the times for her to be a klutz when all she wanted to do was hold her niece until she could see her mommy again. "You will… I promise."

"There's a chair over there." Nick headed toward the empty wheelchair parked next to the nurses' desk. He placed her into the seat as though she were made of china.

She gazed up at him. "Thank you for bringing me. You should go and move your car. The last thing I want is for you to get towed." She smiled. "I'll watch the children."

Nick bent down and hugged his boys. "I'll be right back."

Joy watched as he headed through the doors. She turned at the sound of someone clearing their throat.

"Can I help you?" A petite, redheaded nurse approached with her hands resting on her rounded hips.

"I need to get an X-ray of my foot."

The woman glanced at Joy's ankle, which was growing bigger by the minute and resembling an inflated balloon you might see in a parade. "Oh, my, whatever did you do to yourself?"

"Where's my mommy?" Bella yanked on the nurse's scrubs.

"Excuse me?"

Joy looked up at the nurse. "Her mother, Faith Carlson, was transported here by ambulance earlier."

"Oh, yes. The woman pregnant with twins, right?"

Bella gave the scrubs another tug. "I'm their big sister and I need to see my mommy."

The nurse flashed a sweet smile at the child. "She's with the doctor, but as soon as they get her settled into her room for the evening, you can go back."

Fear ignited in her niece's eyes. "She's not coming home?"

Memories of the fire and the days that followed raced through Joy's mind. Although Bella had been too young to remember when her daddy died, Joy knew she'd heard adults talk about it. Chris had been brought to this hospital, but never returned home. She pulled Bella up onto her lap. "Your mommy will be home before you know it. The doctor probably wants to keep her overnight to make sure the babies are okay."

Joy prayed her words were true. What if Faith lost the twins? She'd already lived through one major loss and that one had nearly broken her.

"I'm going to pray for Mommy and the babies." Bella squeezed her eyes shut and Joy watched her tiny lips move as she prayed in silence.

Moments later, Nick sprinted back into the hospital and looked around with a crinkled brow. "Why haven't you been brought back to X-ray? That foot needs immediate attention!"

His concern warmed her heart, but his slight tantrum made her giggle. "Relax—we were trying to get an update on Faith. As for my foot, I don't think it's that bad."

The nurse handed a clipboard to Joy. "Please fill out the top portion and sign at the bottom. Then we'll take you on back." She looked at Nick. "So your husband can stop worrying."

As Bella and Tyler giggled, Joy noticed Jordan squeezing his eyes shut.

She and Nick exchanged a glance before she spoke up. "He's not my husband. He's just a—"

"I'm a friend. A concerned one, so can we hurry this up?"

Joy passed the completed form back to the nurse.

"Okay, let's go." The woman snatched the paperwork and maneuvered the chair down the hall.

"I'll be right back, Bella. Then we'll see your mommy," Joy yelled over her shoulder as she was pushed through the swinging doors.

"That young man who brought you in sure is handsome." The nurse threw a wink at Joy.

Yes, he was. He'd always been the best-looking man she'd ever laid eyes on. She stared at her foot, praying the pain would cease. But more important, she prayed these feelings for Nick would stop bubbling up inside of her. For years, this had been her prayer, for her love for him to cease, but it seemed she was fighting a losing battle. He had a place burrowed deep within her heart that he refused to leave, but she couldn't—no, she *wouldn't*—allow that to steer her off course from becoming the next principal of Whispering Slopes K-12. Only she wasn't quite sure how to stay on track.

Nick fidgeted in the uncomfortable, dark brown commercial chair lining the brightly painted yellow walls of the hospital's waiting room. The cheery color and the smell of lemony cleaning agents did little to ease his aversion to hospitals. The boys and Bella were entertaining themselves in the play area, alternating between coloring and working a wooden puzzle. Forty-five minutes had passed since Joy went back to X-ray, but still no word. *Lord, please let it be a simple sprain.*

When he opened his eyes, little Bella was standing in front of him with her hands clasped together. "Were you praying, Mr. Nick?"

"Yes, I was. I prayed for your aunt." He smiled.

Tyler walked from the table, leaving Jordan to tackle the puzzle on his own. He climbed into the chair next to his father.

Bella took a seat on the other side. "I've been praying for my mommy, too, but I don't think it's working."

"Why not?" He blinked, confused.

"She hasn't come through the doors. That's what I've been asking God for…to see her." Bella's lower lip trembled.

Tyler leaned over. His brow crinkled. "God always answers our prayers… Maybe He's just real busy."

Nick smiled at his son's response. He put his arm around the frightened little girl.

"You'll see her soon, I promise." Nick spoke with confidence.

Thirty minutes later, after the children had returned to the play area, Nick's heartbeat raced when he spotted Joy coming through the doors into the waiting room. Although on crutches, she approached with swift movements. "Have you heard anything about Faith?"

Bella ran toward her aunt. "When can I see Mommy, Aunt Joy? I need to know she's okay."

Joy placed her crutches onto the tile floor and knelt in front of her niece. "We have to be patient, sweetie. The doctor is doing everything he can to make sure your mommy and the twins are okay." She hugged her tight. "Now, don't you worry one more second. Go play with Tyler and Jordan. I'll be right here if you need me."

She picked up the crutches and turned to Nick. "So any update at all?"

"The nurse said the doctor will be out to speak with you shortly. Like you told Bella, we need to be patient and trust she is in good hands." He stood and guided her to a seat. "You need to sit down and rest. What did the doctor say about your injury?"

"No broken bones." She leaned the crutches against an empty chair and took a seat. "It's only a sprain."

"That's great news. Wearing a cast is the worst… especially when it starts to itch underneath." Nick frowned. "So how long will you have to use those things?" He pointed to the crutches.

"The doctor said about a week, less if the pain subsides sooner." She brushed her hair from her face. "Hopefully I won't be hobbling into my interview."

"Maybe you can use them to your advantage—get the sympathy vote."

Joy's brow furrowed. "What's that supposed to mean?"

Oh, boy, that came out all wrong. He was only joking, but obviously this was a sensitive subject for her. "I'm sorry. I was only playing around."

Her shoulders stiffened. "Do you think that I'm not qualified?"

"That's not what I meant. I just…"

"What? Because I don't have my master's, like you, I'm not ready for the position?" She released a heavy breath. "I've been at that school for ten years. I know it better than anyone."

When would he learn to keep his mouth shut and stop

trying to be the clown? Just like when they were in junior high school and Joy had to get braces on her teeth. Some of the other boys who'd teased him about liking her were calling her Brace Face. At the time, he already had a major crush on her, but he didn't want his friends to know, so he'd joined in on the chanting. As long as he lived, he'd never forget the look on her face when her eyes locked with his before she slammed her locker shut and took off running down the hall. She didn't talk to him for a week. It was the longest seven days of his teenage years.

"Joy, that's not what I meant. It was a poor attempt at trying to be funny. Please, forgive me?" He turned to her, but she continued to stare at the wall opposite their chairs. With their interviews approaching, they were both under pressure. He was sure Joy's level of stress was compounded now that Faith was in the hospital. "Pretty please?"

She attempted to stifle a giggle, but it escaped through her lips. "You're a dork—just like you were in elementary school."

He couldn't argue with that statement. He'd be the first to admit he'd been a little on the nerdy side back then. "Just because someone wears huge Coke-bottle glasses doesn't make them a dork," he laughed.

"What about those silly suspenders?" She chuckled. "Didn't they have little banjos on them?"

When she laughed out loud, the tension in the air seemed to dissolve. This was a good thing.

"I can't believe you remember those." He'd been mortified when his mother made him wear them to school. When he'd arrived that day, he tried taking them off, but his pants kept falling down.

She crinkled up her nose. "Who could forget those

hideous things? You should have put them into the time capsule the class buried."

His face warmed. The capsule… He'd forgotten all about that. Their sixth-grade teacher had asked all of the students to bring in an item or to write a letter and seal it. After everyone placed their contribution into the metal box, it had been buried next to the flagpole. "I couldn't give those away."

"Don't tell me you still have them." She rolled her eyes.

"Of course I do. My grandmother gave them to me when I turned eight years old." He sat up a little straighter.

She laughed. "Whatever you do, don't make the twins wear them. They're still adjusting to a new town and classroom."

"I'm curious—what made you think of the time capsule? I'd forgotten all about it." His mind wandered back to when he'd sat down late on a Sunday night to write his letter to Joy. Since the chances of her ever reading it—or anyone, for that matter—were slim, the twelve-year-old had confessed his love for her. He'd told her he would marry her one day. The feelings in his heart from that night so long ago still fresh, he'd spilled his guts in the letter, believing it would stay in the ground. Life had sure turned out differently from his words written on the paper.

"It's hard to forget when you pass it every day. I remember when Mrs. Willis made a promise that we'd all get together and dig it up in twenty years and share with whomever still lived in town." Her face turned sullen. "She died before we could do it." She picked at her jeans. "Maybe we should do it?"

He turned to her. "Do what?"

"Dig up the box." Her eyes sparkled.

She obviously hadn't buried anything embarrassing. There was no way he'd want her to see what he'd contributed. What would be the point now? Everything between them had been lost. Digging up an old container sure wasn't going to bring anything back. "I don't think that's such a good idea."

"So are you ashamed of what you put into it?" Joy gave him a questioning eye.

"No, of course not."

"Then tell me what it was." She squirmed in her chair.

The fluorescent lighting overhead buzzed and flickered before going dark.

"What fun would that be? Wouldn't you want to be surprised?"

A devious look took hold of her face. "Does that mean you want to do it? It would have to be after school. Maybe we should wait until dark. What do you think?"

She looked way too cute, like an anxious child on Christmas morning. But opening the box could spark a lot of old feelings. How would she feel when she read that he knew he wanted to marry her when he was only in the sixth grade? Was this something he was ready to share with her? "I think we should probably hold off on your little caper for a bit." They both needed more time to get reacquainted. But would that lead him down a path to more pain and suffering for both of them? He didn't have the answers. One thing he did know was that the more time he spent with her the greater the space she took up inside of his heart. This couldn't have been a good thing, not with their pending interviews.

Chapter Eight

Joy's stomach tightened when she hobbled into Faith's hospital room. Her twin's eyes were closed. Good. Her body needed rest. She had one speed: nonstop. Thankfully the doctor had given her something. The more she could sleep during her stay, the better. This was the last place Faith wanted to be. Years ago, she'd spent five endless nights in this hospital before her firefighter husband went to be with the Lord.

Bella was anxious to see her mommy, but the doctor thought it was best to wait. Of course, telling that to a seven-year-old was easier said than done. Joshua was out in the play area with her now, so Joy could have a few moments alone with her sister. Leaning on her crutches, she stood over the bed and watched Faith sleep.

"Why are you hovering?"

Joy practically jumped out of her skin. "You scared me!"

Faith's laugh echoed out the door and down the hall. "That's what you get for watching me like that... Kind of creepy, sis."

"Well, maybe if you didn't do things to freak me out,

like pass out in your office, I wouldn't have to hover."

Joy couldn't imagine a world without her twin. Growing up, they'd done everything together. They were never apart until they went off to different colleges.

"I'm sorry." She gave her sister a once-over. "Wait— what happened? Why are you on crutches?"

Joy waved her hand. "It's no big deal. I just took a little fall. It's only a sprain."

"That's a relief." Faith wiggled herself to sit up. "Is Bella with you? I'd like to see her."

"The doctor wanted you to rest—lie down."

Faith frowned. "I've got too many things to do to rest. So how is Bella? How did she react to me being rushed to the hospital? I'm sure all of this has scared her."

Joy could only dream of ever having the kind of bond Faith had with her child. There was something so special about a mother-and-daughter relationship. Since she and Faith had lost their mother when they were young, and she'd never have children of her own, it would always remain an unattainable dream. "She's dying to see you. I know the doctor said to hold off, but should I go and sneak her in?"

Faith clutched her sister's wrist. "I'd like to talk with you first, if that's okay."

Joy nuzzled up on the edge of the bed. The concerned look on her sister's face made her uneasy. "Of course. Does the doctor know why you passed out?"

Faith nodded. "Yes. Apparently I have a condition called preeclampsia."

Joy had heard of this, but wasn't quite sure how serious it could be. "I think I've read something about this, but I don't remember exactly what it is."

She squeezed Joy's hand. "I know you're a worrywart, but I don't want you to be worried… Promise?"

"Okay."

"It's a condition caused by the pregnancy…or complications, something like that. Anyway, it typically occurs in the third trimester and it causes high blood pressure and elevated protein levels in the urine."

Joy's heart raced. "This sounds pretty serious."

Faith's face turned somber. "It can be."

Why was this happening? Her sister didn't need any more challenges in her life. She'd had enough already. "Is there some medicine he can give to you?"

"The doctor is hopeful that with bed rest, I'll be okay."

Joy's shoulders relaxed at the encouraging news. "Bed rest here or at home?" Joy knew Bella wouldn't take it well if her mommy had to stay here.

"Actually, that's what I wanted to talk with you about. The doctor wants to monitor the babies for a day or two, so that means staying here. You know this is the last place I want to be. There are so many bad memories here, but if it's best for the twins, I've got to stay."

Joy couldn't agree more. If she had her way, she'd want Faith to stay here until she gave birth, but she knew that would probably be impossible. "What do you need me to do?" Faith never liked to ask for help. "Anything. I'm here for you."

"Can Bella stay with you until I come home? It would make it easier on Joshua. He's so busy with the resort. If she stayed with you, he wouldn't have to worry about shuttling her to and from school."

Faith looked pale and so tired.

"Of course." Joy squeezed Faith's hand. "She can stay

with me as long as necessary. Don't you worry at all… Everything will be fine."

The two sisters rested side by side, listening to the sound of a black-capped chickadee chirping on an oak tree outside the window.

Joy sat up a bit and looked at Faith. "Are you scared?"

A tear slipped down her sister's cheek and she nodded. "Yes, but I have to trust God that He'll protect my babies. I think I'm more scared for Joshua. Since I told him I was pregnant, I've never seen him this happy. He's always wanted children. I want to give him that gift."

Joy recalled when they were in the third grade and both had come down with strep throat. Their grandmother had sent them straight to bed, but Faith kept sneaking outside. She said she didn't feel bad and she was bored. Joy had followed her grandmother's instructions, and once better she'd ended up visiting Faith in the hospital, after she'd ended up with pneumonia. "You will, but you'll have to follow the doctor's orders. I know that you don't like to lie around. But please, promise me, for the sake of your twins and your own health, you'll follow his recommendations."

"Of course I will." She rubbed her belly. "Could you bring Bella back? I need to see that sweet little face."

Joy kissed her sister's cheek. "You got it. After you visit, we'll head back to the Black Bear and help out the staff with the remaining activities."

Faith smiled. "Joshua would really appreciate that. I'd like for him to get back, too, but I have a feeling he's going to want to stay here, which really isn't necessary."

She was fully aware of Joshua's feelings for her twin. She and Bella were his world. He'd always put his family before business. "Well, you know that's not going to happen, so don't try to fight it. I'll take care of everything. You rest and let your husband spoil you and those precious babies."

Joy reached for her crutches leaning against the bed. She stood and her shoulders dropped a notch. Her sister was so blessed. To have a man who put his wife before his own wants and feelings was a rare find. At least it'd always been for her. "I'll go get Bella."

She kissed her sister's forehead and slowly hobbled out of the room. Despite lying in a hospital bed, she thought her twin was the most blessed woman she knew.

Twenty minutes later, Joy spotted Joshua and Bella coming down the hallway. After visiting with Faith she'd taken her seat back in the waiting room in order to get off the crutches. Nick had been quite concerned about her sister's condition and offered to help in any way. For the past ten minutes, he'd been in the play area entertaining his boys, who were already missing Bella.

"Come see the puzzle, Bella!" Tyler shouted when the twins spotted her skipping down the hall.

Her niece grinned from ear to ear. That was a good sign.

Before heading to the playroom, the little girl stopped by Joy's chair.

"Mommy's going to stay here for a little while so the babies can get better, but she said I can stay at your house." A huge smile spread across her face. "Can we invite Jordan and Tyler over for a cookout and to watch a movie tonight?"

Bella's voice carried across the room and undoubtedly straight into Nick's ears. He turned at the mention of his boys. Of course, the twins heard and immediately jumped to their feet. "Oh, can we, Daddy, please?" both cried out.

A solemn Joshua stood quietly and observed.

Joy had been afraid this would happen. With Bella staying at her house and being so close in proximity to the boys, it was only natural they'd want to play together. "We'll talk about it. Why don't you go over with the others so I can speak with your father?"

Bella scampered across the room.

"You okay?" Joy reached out for her brother-in-law's hand.

His boots clanked against the tile as he approached. He raked his hand across his face before reaching for hers. "That woman is amazing. She's the one in the hospital, but she's comforting me. I could barely hold it together back there."

"That's because you're a great husband. Thank you for being so good to my sister."

He sucked in a deep breath and then released. "If anything happens to her or the twins, I don't know what I'll do." He sank down into the empty chair next to hers and covered his face with his hands.

She reached over and rubbed his back. "You know my sister is as tough as they come. Those babies are going to be safe—she'll make sure of it."

"Did she tell you the doctor might have to induce labor early if they can't get her blood pressure down?"

Faith hadn't mentioned it, perhaps in hopes that if she didn't, it wouldn't come to fruition. "Even if she's induced, she's far enough along the twins would be okay. Please, don't worry. Just pray. Our grandmother always taught us that prayer was powerful—it changes things." As she spoke the words her mamaw preached,

Joy wasn't quite sure this applied to her. There'd been a lot of things she'd prayed for, but she always seemed to be left waiting.

The two sat in silence for a couple of moments until Nick approached.

He extended his hand to Joshua. "I'm sorry, man. Please, let me know if there's anything I can do."

Joshua gripped the hand and rose to his feet. "Thanks, bud. Right now, I don't know what end is up, but I appreciate it."

Joy had been around the resort enough to know the daily operation. Plus, with the top-notch staff, they'd keep things running smoothly. "Since I know you're not going to leave your wife's side, let me take Bella and we'll go back to the Black Bear. I can handle the awards ceremony set for later this evening and wrap things up. Plus, there's a lot of the school faculty there to help, too."

Joshua shook his head. "Oh, I was so concerned about Faith, I completely forgot about the ceremony."

"It's all handled. You stay here and take care of my sister."

Nick looked at Joy and then to Joshua. "I'll help her. Don't worry about a thing."

The children ran to the adults. "We'll help, too, Mr. Joshua," Tyler added. "We love Ms. Kelliher and Bella, too."

Joy's heart melted at Jordan and Tyler's declaration. But was this a good idea? The more attached the boys got, the harder it would be to deal with the fallout once the principal position was filled. She couldn't think about that now. She'd need all the help she could get to keep the resort and Bella's life running as normal as possible. She looked at her brother-in-law. "See, we've got it covered."

* * *

With the kids safely buckled in, Nick and Joy secured their belts. He slid the key into the ignition and turned the switch. Pressing the accelerator, Nick drove the SUV out of the hospital parking lot and onto the winding mountain road.

Joy had been quiet since he'd offered to help out at the resort. It was the right thing to do. He'd always cared for Faith and now her family needed assistance. For now, he and Joy would have to act like grown-ups and put their individual beliefs of who would be the best person for the principal position aside.

As the kids chattered in the back seat, Nick eased the accelerator when he reached a stop sign. He turned to Joy, who appeared lost in thought as she gazed out the passenger window.

"You okay?"

She nodded. "I'm just worried."

He knew her mind was heavy with concern for Faith. "She's tough. Your sister and the babies will be fine. Right now she's in the best place she can be and her husband is there with her."

Nick's stomach twisted at his words and guilt crept in. Joshua was a much better husband than he'd ever been. He hadn't been there for his wife when she needed him. As far as he was concerned, he was a pretty poor excuse for a man. What would Joy think if she knew the truth? Would she be thankful that his family had left and she'd never married him as they'd planned?

"Look at all of the deer, Daddy."

Tyler's announcement broke the silence that hung between the two adults.

Nick turned the wheel and safely glided the SUV

over to the shoulder of the road so all of the passengers could take in the beautiful sight. He gazed out to the open meadow and was amazed by the number of deer grazing. "I don't think I've ever seen that many."

Joy smiled. "They know they're safe there since it's part of the Shenandoah National Park."

Bella had her nose pressed to the window. "They're so pretty. They remind me of my mommy. She's pretty, too, and she loves to watch the deer." She sighed. "I miss her."

"I miss our mommy, too," Tyler said.

Nick eyed his sons in the rearview mirror. His boys were left heartbroken after the death of their mother—a death that could have been prevented had he not been so selfish. The brief period of joy brought about by the deer faded as he put the car into Drive and slowly pulled away.

Ten minutes later when he turned into the entrance of the Black Bear, the grounds still buzzed with activity. Nick rounded to the other side of the car to open the door for Joy. The children hopped out while he pulled the crutches from the floor of the back seat.

As they headed toward the main house, a tall, slender blonde woman ran toward them. "Oh, no! Is it broken?"

"No, thankfully it's only a minor sprain," Joy answered with an eye roll.

The woman embraced Joy. "That's good to hear. How's Faith? I've been so worried."

"It's not good for you to worry, Sherida. She'll be okay, but she has to stay in the hospital for a bit."

Sherida pulled away. "I want you and your sister's family to be reassured that the staff and I have everything under control."

"I know you do, and we all appreciate it." Joy focused her attention on Nick. "I apologize for my rudeness. Sherida, this is Nick Capello and his boys, Tyler and Jordan."

The boys smiled and Nick extended his hand. "It's nice to meet you."

He knew the name. Faith and Joshua's employee—the one living with Crohn's disease, but she looked healthy. How could that be? Sherida didn't look anything like his wife had before she died. The last couple of months of her life, Michelle had been so thin and without color. Why hadn't he noticed it until it was too late?

Sherida's touch was gentle when she placed her hand in his. "It's nice to meet you," she said softly. "Thank you so much for coming and bringing your adorable boys. Joshua, Faith and the entire staff have worked so hard on this event. It's wonderful to see such a great turnout, especially since so many are donating to the Crohn's and Colitis Foundation. I've been completely overwhelmed by the support of the community." Sherida smiled.

Joy stepped closer and placed her hand on Sherida's forearm. "According to my sister, if it weren't for you the Black Bear would have never survived its first few months." She turned to Nick. "Sherida was their first official hire when they opened. She has superb marketing skills. In fact, last month it was named one of the top inns in the state."

"We're all a team here." Sherida beamed.

Nick noticed the redness that dotted her cheeks. Obviously the woman was quite humble.

"How have you been feeling?" Joy asked.

"Since I've been on this new medication, I feel fantastic. I wish this drug had been around ten years ago. It would have saved me a lot of suffering."

Nick wrung his hands together. If only he'd paid attention to his wife, he could have gotten her on this medication. Sherida looked like the picture of health.

"That's great news," Joy said. "Since Joshua won't be back at the inn this evening, we wanted to see if there's anything we can do to help."

Sherida glanced at the children, who were running in circles trying to keep themselves entertained. "It looks like you both have your hands full with those three. I've got plenty of help, so don't worry about anything. Go along and enjoy your evening. Besides, a lot of the teachers have already left. You've done your duty here," she softly insisted.

Joy hugged Sherida. "Just call if you need anything. Bella and I will swing by tomorrow."

They said their goodbyes and the group strolled toward the parking lot.

"Can we grill hamburgers and hot dogs on your firepit, Aunt Joy?"

Nick looked at Joy with an arched brow. He knew the kids had probably cooked up this plan while they were working on the puzzle back at the hospital. He hated to disappoint them, but an evening with Joy probably wasn't a good idea.

"It looks as though our night has been planned. Are you okay with it?" Joy asked as she adjusted her crutches under her arm.

"Sure, it's okay, isn't it, Daddy?" Tyler spoke out. "Besides, you make the best burgers in the world."

Didn't he get a vote? Nick's stomach twisted, but he'd have to do what was best for his boys. They deserved to have as much fun as they could today. Truth be told, he was a little surprised she agreed to the plan, especially after he'd put his foot in his mouth while they were at the hospital. "Okay, let's head back to the house." He turned to Joy.

"What about my clothes, Aunt Joy? And my teddy bear… I can't sleep without him."

"Oh, I wasn't even thinking. I'm glad you mentioned your things, sweetie." She faced Nick. "You and the twins go ahead. Bella and I can meet you at the house, since my tire has been fixed."

"You sure you're okay to drive on that foot?" Nick could sense his protective instincts taking hold.

Joy laughed. "I don't use my left foot to drive, silly."

Right… What was he thinking? He knew what he was thinking. He was excited to have more time with Joy. "I guess you're right. Would you like for me and the boys to stop at the store on the way over?" he offered.

"Let's all ride together to the market. I have a few things I need to pick up, along with the items for the cookout."

Nick watched as Joy hobbled along on the crutches toward Bella's house. He wondered how different his life would be if his father hadn't moved his family to Chicago. Would he and Joy have gone ahead with their plans to marry? What about now? If he ever thought about remarrying, could he have a future with Joy? His throat grew thick. Who was he kidding—he wasn't husband material. She deserved much better than a man like him.

Chapter Nine

A half an hour later, Joy had returned to her house and everyone was congregated on the driveway. The children were bursting with anticipation of an evening spent together. Joy had mixed feelings. Why had she agreed to this get-together? Was she doing it for the children or did she deep down want to spend more time with Nick?

"Is everyone ready to head out to the grocery store to get what we need?" Nick glanced up at the sky. "It looks like it'll be a perfect evening for a cookout—crisp, but not too cold, if we all bundle up."

The weather was perfect. With a few clouds rolling in from the west, they'd serve as a cozy blanket to keep the nighttime temperature from dropping too low.

"This is going to be a great night," Jordan cheered.

For years, Joy spent Saturday nights alone, usually doing her laundry and making up her grocery shopping list so she could hit the market after Sunday services. The thought of a house full of guests and ignoring the pile of clothes in need of laundering created a sense of excitement. Her heart squeezed as she studied Nick attending to his boys. The love in his eyes exploded. He really was a wonderful father. A wave of sadness washed over her as she thought about how different their lives could have been and how simple choices in life could alter the outcome.

Nick opened the passenger-side door and helped her climb aboard. He reached for Joy's crutches and stowed them inside the trunk.

With the kids all loaded they set off for the market, and Joy's shoulders relaxed. Was this what it was like to be a family? Maybe just for tonight, she could pretend that was exactly what they were—a happy family just enjoying the evening. She and Nick were husband and wife and they were going grocery shopping with their children. It was a lovely thought, but not reality.

"Daddy, wuh like a family, awen't we?"

Joy flinched. It was as though Jordan had read her mind. Her cheeks warmed as she glanced in Nick's direction. He maintained his focus on the road and appeared completely unaffected by his son's comment. Or was he simply ignoring it?

Was that why she felt safe? Like the herd of deer they'd seen earlier in the meadow. Protected. For the first time since childhood, she'd allowed herself to feel like part of a family and it felt good…really good. Wait, she couldn't—it would never happen. She had to rid her mind of these crazy thoughts. They were doing this for the children. There was nothing more to it. But why did she feel like a high school girl who had just been invited to the prom by her secret crush?

An hour later, back from their shopping trip, Joy's kitchen smelled of lemongrass, thanks to her aromatherapy diffuser she'd plugged in ten minutes earlier. As the sun slowly dipped behind the mountains, Joy pressed the hamburger meat with the palm of her hand and carefully shaped it into perfectly rounded patties. Outside, flames danced in the firepit, thanks to Nick. She watched as he meticulously cleaned the grill. It was nice to have a man around the house to take care of such things, even if it was only for tonight.

A smile tugged on her lips as contentment filled her heart. At that moment, she longed to talk to her sister about the array of emotions bubbling inside of her. She knew Faith would tell her to relax and enjoy the company of Nick and the boys. *Stay in the moment*, her sister always said, but that was easier said than done. So much hurt still lingered from the past. Joy knew it was the Christian thing to do to forgive Nick for moving. For years, she'd studied forgiveness, trying to work through her pain. Knowing what she knew now, how could she continue to blame him? His mother had been ill and his father only did what he'd thought best for the family. Still, what happened after he'd left was where she struggled. But did Nick deserve all of the blame? She forced those thoughts out of her head and gazed out the window. The children played a game of tag and were enjoying life, as children did. A yard full of kids of her own—it was what her heart desired. That, along with the principal position, would make her life perfect. Wouldn't it?

"Aunt Joy, don't forget the extra cheese for the burgers. You know I love it, just like you." Bella skipped into the kitchen through the patio door with her hair up in lopsided ponytails. Her red winter coat completely unzipped and her pullover knit sweater hiked up, exposing her little belly.

"Oh, I know. I won't forget." Joy turned on the faucet and washed her hands in warm soapy water. "Do you want me to fix your hair? I think the pony rides were a little rough."

Bella grabbed hold of the elastic bands and pulled them loose, sending her hair cascading to her shoulders. "No, thank you. My hair hurts from these things." She handed the bands to her aunt.

Joy chuckled. "I'll put these with your overnight bag. Before you go back outside, please zip up your coat. I don't want you getting sick."

"But it's warm by the fire." She turned to go back outside but stopped abruptly. "Oh, yeah, I forgot. Uncle Nick wanted to know if you'd like for him to sweep the patio before he starts to cook."

Uncle. Had her niece taken it upon herself to call Nick her uncle? Or even worse, had he suggested it? The latter made her feel a little unsettled. She needed to know.

"Sweetie, did Mr. Nick ask you to call him Uncle?"

Bella shook her head. "No, but if he was, that would mean you guys are married. I thought I'd pretend...just for tonight." She studied her aunt. "Is that okay?"

Joy headed to the pantry and grabbed the broom. She handed it to her niece. "Well, just don't say it in front of him."

"I already did." Bella snatched the sweeper. "I think he liked it." She grinned.

She shot out the door, leaving Joy speechless. Could that be true? Did the idea of him being an uncle to Bella make her happy? A slight twinge of excitement shuddered down her spine at the possibilities. No. These were crazy thoughts. There was no future when it came to her and Nick. But what if his father hadn't withheld the letters and Nick had tried to come back sooner...before he'd met the boys' mother? Maybe she wouldn't have had to carry this secret alone her entire life. She shook her head. Playing the what-if game wasn't a good idea.

Despite her best efforts, her mind continued to wander, thinking of what might have been until her arm accidentally brushed the platter of hamburger patties. She tossed her crutches aside and tried to snatch the plate, but it flew off the counter and onto the hardwood floor.

Crash.

A sea of crumbled meat surrounded her feet. Thankfully, the plate was made of plastic and not glass. She reached for the paper towels and yanked a handful from the holder.

"Joy!" Nick came bursting through the patio doorway. "Are you okay?"

Her hair hung in her face as she hopped on one foot to grab more paper towels. "I'm fine, but I'm afraid our dinner is splattered all over the floor."

He rushed to her and reached for her hands. "You didn't cut yourself, did you?"

Her face warmed. What a complete klutz. She always knew she was worthless in the kitchen. How much practice could you get cooking for one? "No, it's plastic."

Joy got down on her knees with the towels. When Nick knelt beside her, she inhaled a spicy whiff of cologne that caused her head to swirl like a merry-go-round in overdrive. He smelled like nutmeg and some other spice she couldn't quite place. She didn't want to admit it, but it was a balm for her frazzled nerves.

"What a mess. I'm so sorry."

"No harm done. As clean as your floor looks, we'll just follow the five-second rule. With a quick rinse of the meat and a little re-forming, we'll get these patties back into shape and out on the grill." He flashed a smile.

Their hands brushed when they both reached for the same piece of meat. They paused and their eyes locked for a moment. Heat crept up the back of her neck.

"Why don't you go outside and sit down. You've been on that ankle too much today." His voice was gentle. "I'll take care of this."

Joy pushed herself off the floor. As she held on to the edge of the countertop, Nick got to his feet and retrieved her crutches.

"You're going to need these." He passed them to her with a wink.

Her insides turned to mush. As she worked her way toward the back door, she cast a longing gaze over her shoulder, watching while Nick cleaned up her mess. She found comfort in the way he took control of the situation and his obvious concern for her well-being, but she had to shove away the warm thoughts as she moved briskly toward the door. They were only together tonight for the children—she knew that, but why did she have to keep reminding herself? She had to guard her heart. When her hand gripped the cool metal doorknob she wondered… were they really spending time together just because of the children?

Nick blew out a heavy breath when the patio door closed. Talk about sparks. His pulse had raced a mile a minute when their hands had brushed. He'd come close to whisking her into his arms. Okay, so maybe that was just a fantasy. He knew how she felt toward him for a multitude of reasons. The biggest one was the fact that there was one position and two applicants. But hadn't there been times when her eyes looked warm and open to something more? Or was he living in a fantasy world?

He busied himself cleaning the floor, trying to peel Joy out of his brain. Heading toward the sink, he turned on the faucet and gave the meat a quick rinse under some cold water. After blotting it with paper towels, he re-formed the patties to their original shape and applied the seasoning. There, that wasn't that big of a deal. But Joy seemed to think it was. She appeared to get stressed easily. Perhaps she was worried about Faith, but now that he thought about it, even before she went into the hospital, he'd noticed there was something different about her. Sure, there was that tough exterior she wore, but below, at times she almost seemed skittish, like a barn-yard cat. Shoving the package of hot dogs under his arm, he grabbed the plate of burgers and gripped it tight.

Outside, Nick took in a deep breath of the crisp January night air. The air in Chicago didn't come close to creating the invigorating sensation Nick felt when he breathed in here. "Is everyone warm enough?" he asked as he watched the children enjoying the fire. "If you want to wait inside, I'll have the food ready soon." He inhaled deeply, enjoying the scent of pine that permeated the air.

Tyler darted toward his father. "Daddy, it's warm by the firepit." He turned on his heel and rejoined his playmates.

Nick set the plate on the grill's side table. "Okay, but these will cook in no time." He slid the patties one at a time over the dancing flame.

Joy grabbed her crutches and came to Nick's side as the kids chattered among themselves.

"Hey, look out there." Nick pointed to the open field behind her house. "Do you know what that reminds me of?"

She shook her head. "Not really."

"Remember when we were kids and we'd go to the Lancasters' field and catch fireflies?"

He opened the package of hot dogs and lined six on the grill.

She smiled and gazed out into the darkness. "I'd forgotten about that."

"Timmy Biddle called you the firefly whisperer. After we counted to determine the winner, you'd make everyone immediately set them free."

Joy laughed. "I didn't want them to suffocate."

"That's why we punched holes in the lid, silly." He gave her a playful nudge with his left arm.

"I know, but I felt sorry for them. They weren't meant to be kept in a jar. Sometimes, when I felt lonely and was desperately missing my parents, their light was the only thing I saw when I looked out of my bedroom window. They made me feel safe." Still focused on the open space, she fingered her gold chain.

"That's important to you, isn't it?"

She turned to him. "What?"

"Feeling safe."

"Yes, I guess so. After my parents were killed and I was a few years older, I remember being afraid of everything. Mostly I was scared something would happen to my grandparents and Faith and I would end up in an orphanage." She half smiled. "Sounds kind of silly, doesn't it?"

"No, not to a child." He carefully slid the spatula underneath a burger and flipped it onto its other side. The splattering grease hissed like a snake ready to strike. "When my mother got sick, I remember thinking all kinds of crazy thoughts. My father had been so stressed.

I thought he'd walk out on his family—leaving me and my sister alone to care for his addicted wife."

Joy looked up at him. Her hazel eyes twinkled in the moonlight. "That must have been a scary time for you."

The mournful sound of a train's whistle sounded in the distance. He nodded, but remained silent and returned his attention to the grill as Joy hobbled back to the fire.

Ten minutes later, Nick placed the last patty on the ceramic platter. "I'm afraid it's getting a little too cold out here for you guys. We should probably eat in the house. What do you think?" He turned to Joy and got his answer. She looked frozen. Snuggled with the throw blanket that once had been neatly folded on the back of the chair, she nodded.

"Definitely—inside." Her teeth chattered.

The group herded inside and the kids plopped down at the kitchen table.

Joy placed one hand on her hip. "Did you all forget something?"

The children looked at each other and then shrugged.

"Grace?" Tyler asked.

Nick walked over with an oven mitt and gently tapped it on his son's head. "Well, yes, but first go wash up." He wiggled his hands in the air.

In an instant the sound of three chairs scraping across the hardwood floor filled the room. The kids headed to the sink to clean their hands.

Joy gave Nick an eye roll.

"Don't forget the soap," he added, knowing his boys were famous for doing a quick swipe under the water.

With everyone seated at the table, Joy turned to Bella. "Would you say grace, please?"

Bella bowed her head along with the others.

"Dear Lord, thank You for this yummy meal and for Jordan and Tyler. Oh, and don't let the principal job make Aunt Joy and Uncle Nick fight. I don't want to lose my new friends. Amen."

Silence surrounded the table until Tyler turned to his father. "You're not going to get into a fight with my teacher, are you, Daddy?" His cheeks flushed as he tipped his chin toward his plate.

"Bella, what would make you pray for such a thing?" Joy asked, strumming her fingers along the tabletop.

"I heard you talking to my mommy about it. You both really want the job, but there's only one." Bella took a bite of her burger.

"I think my daddy will get it," Tyler announced. "Boys make better principals. Right, Daddy?"

Bella slapped her bun back on the plate and pouted her lower lip. "That's not true. Girls can do anything boys can. Right, Aunt Joy?"

Nick's jaw tensed. This conversation was headed in the wrong direction and it needed to stop. He didn't want the job opening to create a rift between the children.

Joy leaned back in her chair and crossed her arms. "Yes, Bella, we can do anything that boys can do. And don't ever let anyone tell you otherwise."

"Tyler, please apologize for your comment," Nick said.

"I'm sorry, Bella. I didn't mean to hurt your feelings," Tyler said. His lower lip quivered as he turned to Joy. "I'm sorry, Miss Kelliher."

Relief settled in when Joy's shoulders seemed to relax and she leaned forward. She reached for Tyler's hand. "I know you didn't, sweetie."

The adults finished their meal in silence while the children debated which game they'd play after dinner.

"May we be excused, Aunt Joy?" Bella asked as she wiped a dollop of ketchup off her chin.

The boys looked at their father.

Joy nodded. "Yes, you may. You all go ahead and play a game until I get the dishes finished."

Nick noticed she had glanced his way to include him. Obviously she didn't want any help in the kitchen, but he wasn't going to stand for that.

With enthusiasm, the kids headed for the family room. Nick reached for his plate and strolled toward the sink.

Abandoning her crutches, Joy jumped up and headed him off. "I'll take that. You go on and play with them."

She was as stubborn as they came and so cute, too. Two could play this game. Nick gripped the plate as she continued this match of tug-of-war.

"Let go."

He bit his lip to keep from smiling. She was serious, but so was he. "Hey, you insisted on helping when you came to my house—it's only fair."

Joy's hand dropped to her side. "Fine—even though you didn't let me help." She reached for the twins' plates.

Nick turned on the faucet to let the water warm. Joy stepped beside him, carrying two plates. He took the dishes and their fingers brushed. "Look, I'm really sorry about what Tyler said."

Her shoulders shrugged. "He's just a child, but I certainly hope that's not the kind of talk he hears around the house." She attacked the yellow plate with the scrubber.

Seriously? Didn't she know that wasn't the kind of man he was? Of course she didn't. He'd been a kid when he'd left. She didn't know anything about the man he'd grown up to be. "Absolutely not. My boys are being raised to respect women and to know both men and women can do anything they want in this world."

Outside, a deluge of rain pounded against the window. The northwesterly wind battered the shudders. It had been a wise decision to come inside to eat.

Joy turned off the water. "I know. I'm sorry. I've been so stressed lately. I suppose I'm taking it out on you."

"So, tell me what's bothering you. The job, Faith, or is it my presence?"

She blew out a heavy breath and raked her hands through her hair. "It's everything. I know it's silly of me to think I could be a shoo-in for the job, but before you came back to town, I really thought it would be mine. Let's not talk about this. We want the children to enjoy their evening."

The rain pecked against the gutters as Joy turned her attention back to the sink.

Nick headed to the table to clear some more dishes when he caught a glimpse of *The Whispering Slopes Gazette* lying on the antique white buffet. He smiled as he lifted the paper. "Boy, this sure brings back a lot of memories."

"What does?" Joy asked as she wiped down the stainless-steel pot with a dish towel.

Nick slipped back into his chair and skimmed through the pages of the publication. "The newspaper… It's been years since I've seen a copy. I must have pedaled my bicycle for hundreds of miles when I delivered this as a young boy."

She turned, wearing a smile. "I remember Mrs. Morris always yelled at you for throwing the paper in her flower garden," Joy added.

He'd forgotten about that and the reminder made him smile. "Yeah, my aim wasn't the best, but I had to stay on schedule. I only had an hour to deliver through the entire town. I didn't want to be late to school."

As he turned to page three, his eye caught the headline, "Whispering Slopes Former Star Quarterback Killed in Boating Accident."

"Joy, did you see this article?"

She turned slightly as she loaded the silverware in the dishwasher. "No, I haven't had a chance to look at the paper today."

"Remember Scotty Brammer, the star quarterback of our high school?"

Nick flinched at the loud clattering of dishes. "You okay over there?" He stared over his shoulder and observed Joy with her hands clutched to the corner of the countertop.

"I—I'm fine. What about him?"

He turned his attention back to the article. "He was killed in a boating accident in Fort Lauderdale, Florida. It also says he'd been awaiting trial— This is unbelievable."

"What is it, Nick? What does it say?"

"Apparently he'd been accused of assaulting a student at the school where he worked as the girls' soccer coach."

Before Nick knew what was happening, Joy bolted across the room and snatched the paper from his hands.

"Let me see!" she exclaimed and took an empty seat.

Nick watched the blood drain from her face. Her hands shook violently as her eyes scanned the page.

"No!" Joy screamed and shoved away from the table.

She headed toward the back door and took off into the cold rain, leaving her crutches behind.

Why on earth was she reacting this way? Had there been something personal between Joy and Scotty after he'd left town? He grabbed his coat from the foyer closet and yelled toward the family room. "Kids, I'll be right back." Nick slid his arms into the sleeves of his leather jacket. Outside, the inky sky released icy drops of rain that peppered his face. His feet skidded under slushy leaves as he went in search of Joy and answers.

Chapter Ten

Fat raindrops splattered against Joy's face as her pace slowed to a limp. Ignoring the pain, she continued to move down the coal-black path toward the shed. The Ace bandage around her foot, now caked with mud, loosened with each step. The piercing pain shooting through her ankle couldn't compare to how she'd felt when Nick had read the article about Scotty.

Memories of the night Nick had left town bubbled to the surface. A young girl so scared and feeling alone in the world. Why had she gotten into the car with Scotty? She'd been angry with Nick, but was that reason enough to have such poor judgment? Hadn't she smelled alcohol on his breath?

Why are You allowing this to happen, Lord?

What was she thinking? He didn't allow this—she did. She'd made the life-changing decision that night. And now because of her reckless actions, another young girl had been attacked—maybe more. Why hadn't she gone to the police? She could have spared this child the pain. Now the girl would endure the same everlasting shame that hung like a low-lying fog over a mountain valley…for the rest of her life.

Joy yanked open the shed's cedar door, entered, then pulled it closed with hopes of trapping the memories on the other side of the wall, but they were forever singed inside the layers of her brain. Reaching for the lock, she remembered it was broken—just one of a million other things on her list in need of attention. Everything had gone on the back burner until she finished up her master's studies. Soaking wet, she dropped to the floor between the lawn mower and large sacks of potting soil. She inhaled the scent of cedar and her grandfather's face flashed through her mind. He'd always smelled like it. Through the sounds of the howling wind, she heard Nick's voice calling out for her.

"Joy! Are you in there?"

No. Don't come in here, Nick. I'm too ashamed to share this with you.

The doorknob turned and she wanted to disappear between the cracks of the dusty wooden floor. The door squeaked as he pushed it open and a gust of wind blasted into the room. Her world spiraled out of control. Everything she'd tried to keep secret would be exposed if he came inside. She brushed the wet matted hair away from her eyes. The swishing of his jeans sounded and then his muddy shoes stood in front of her.

"Please… I'm begging you, Nick—go away."

He knelt, his face washed with concern. "Joy, tell me what's wrong. I want to help you." Despite the cold rain, his hand felt warm when he placed it on her cheek. Her heart gave a little leap as old feelings simmered inside, but she quickly attempted to push them away.

"You can't help me—no one can." The tears streamed

down her cheeks. She swallowed hard, remembering that night. "You're too late. Don't you see?" She wanted to turn back the clock, erase that evening from her past.

He ran his hands through his rain-soaked hair as he studied her in search of an answer. "Late? For what?" He took a seat next to her and stared at the side of her face. "Why did you react to the article that way? Did you date Scotty after I left?"

Her blood froze at the sound of his name. Date? "No!" The young man who'd turned her world upside down and transformed her into a woman who found it impossible to trust men. She'd never been able to have a lasting relationship, mainly because she felt unworthy—broken— used. "Nick, I'm begging you—please don't mention him to me…ever." Her shoulders quivered.

Nick placed his hands on her arms. "What on earth is going on? I want to help you, but I can't if you don't open up to me."

A howling wind rattled the shingles on the roof as his eyes pleaded for an answer.

"Come on, Joy. It's me, Nick."

She lifted her eyes and held his gaze. Could he help her? Her heart said yes, but would telling him shatter what was left of their relationship? The salty tears ran into the corners of her mouth. She raked the back of her hand across her lips. "That night…you were supposed to meet me."

"I know, and I'm so sorry I wasn't there. My father picked me up after work. He had the car all packed and we headed straight for Chicago."

If she'd meant anything to him, he would have insisted his father bring him to the pond—if only to say goodbye. "But if you'd at least come by...he wouldn't have..."

"He, who? Talk. I can help."

Her words strangled her breath and she coughed. Shaking, she wrapped her arms around her chest, unable to tell him the events of the night. She couldn't go down that dark road.

"I'm not leaving until you tell." He pressed his back against the cedar wall.

She sucked in a deep breath and released. "It doesn't matter anymore."

"You're so upset. Of course it does."

"You weren't there for me and that's a fact that will never change."

"You're right—I wasn't there, but I'm here now. Tell me...is this all because I left without saying goodbye?" His question echoed.

If only it were that simple. She wiped her cheeks with the back of each hand. "We've got to get back inside with the children." She had to break free from his questions.

"They're working a puzzle and watching *Willy Wonka and the Chocolate Factory*. They'll be fine."

She'd carried this secret for so many years, it had left her physically and mentally exhausted. Was this the reason God had brought him back to Whispering Slopes, so she'd no longer have to carry this weight? Keeping it bottled up had only made her feel like a pressure cooker, ready to explode. "The night, at the pond, I waited for you..." Chills ran down her back as she recalled the sound of leaves crunching. Footsteps. It was her one and only love, coming to meet her, just as he'd promised. But when she'd turned, the smile she'd worn all evening had slid from her face.

"Go on." Nick leaned toward her.

Bile moved up in the back of her throat. "I heard someone coming." She recalled the thick cloud cover that hung low that evening. "It was so dark, but I assumed it was you—since you promised to meet me."

"Joy...who was it?"

She hesitated, then turned away quickly before dry heaving into her hand.

Silence consumed the cold and damp shed.

"Scotty," she whispered.

"Was he meeting Lisa?"

Joy had thought the same thing when he'd appeared out of nowhere. Lisa was the captain of the cheerleading squad and his longtime girlfriend. They'd been going together since freshman year. Of course that was who he'd be meeting—or so she'd thought.

"Joy? Was Lisa at the pond, too?"

She could only shake her head. The shame that weighed on her shoulders felt like she'd been treading water for years in the middle of the ocean with a life jacket made of lead. She inhaled a deep breath and released. "I'd waited for over an hour. I was angry at you for not showing up. It had started to rain when Scotty asked if I wanted to go get a slice of pizza." Joy wiped a tear that ran down her cheek. "We walked to his car. I got inside. It was my fault."

Joy flinched when Nick's hand rested on her shoulder.

"It was only pizza, Joy. Besides, I left you waiting. I don't blame you for going with Scotty... Just forget about it." He got to his feet and reached for her hand. "Come on. Let's go back to the house."

She jerked her hand free. "I can't forget, Nick. I smelled the alcohol on his breath, but I still went with him."

Nick dropped back to his knees, and his brow crinkled. "He'd been drinking?"

Joy shivered as she recalled how hurt she'd been. Once inside Scotty's car, she'd buckled her seat belt, hoping Nick would show up and find her gone. "I wanted to get back at you."

"What happened, Joy?"

After all these years, the sound of Scotty's windshield wipers swishing against the window as he drove past the Pizza Shack remained fresh in her mind. "He didn't take me out for pizza." Her eyes peppered with more tears as she wrapped her arms around her waist, willing that horrible night from her head. "He drove to the old McAllister farm." She remembered his cold and glassy eyes, filled with hate, as Scotty told her Lisa had broken up with him.

"The McAllisters'? That place had been abandoned for—"

Unable to make eye contact with Nick, Joy stared at the cedar floor, emotionless. Her only love, he'd never think the same of her again.

With a swift movement, she was in his arms. She knew then that he'd realized what had happened to her.

"I'm so sorry, Joy," he sobbed.

Nick wouldn't let go, and for the first time since that night, she felt safe. His embrace was a balm to her wounded heart.

His face buried into her shoulder. "I should have been there. If I had, this never would have happened."

She pulled away and eyed his red, splotchy face. A part of her was relieved he knew, but had she been wrong to put this guilt on him after all these years? He couldn't have known what was going to happen. Besides, he had to go with his family. His father needed him. Joy shook her head. "No, I made the decision to get in the car with Scotty. I have only myself to blame."

They sat in silence for a moment as Nick ran his fingers through her damp, tangled hair.

"I'm so sorry this happened to you, Joy."

"I know you are. But it's all in the past. Time heals—isn't that what they say?" She hadn't healed. Instead, she'd become an expert at compartmentalizing. She'd placed those memories into a special box and shoved it to the far corner of her mind. She'd never sought professional help to deal with the events of that night. What was the point? She'd made the choice that would define who she was for the rest of her life.

"Did you go to the police?"

Pieces of the night flickered in her mind. Scotty had driven her home. Neither had spoken a word, until he pulled up to the curb in front of her house. "See you in school on Monday." His words held no remorse. The hours that followed she had stood in the shower, fully clothed, and had desperately willed the water to wash away the horrific events of the evening. She'd scrubbed until she thought her skin would bleed, but she couldn't make herself pure like the girl she'd been when she woke up that morning. "No, I was too ashamed." When Joy had seen Scotty the next day in school, he'd threatened to spread rumors about her. How she'd been the one who came on to him, not the other way around. No one would believe her. He'd been the most popular kid in school. "I just wanted it all to go away."

He placed his hand under her chin and tilted her head. "Thank you for sharing this with me. I know it couldn't have been easy for you, but you've got to stop blam-

ing yourself. Scotty was intoxicated. You had no way
of knowing he'd be capable of something so horrific."

"I know it wasn't his character. He'd been voted Best
All-Around our junior year. Do you remember?"

Nick nodded as he tucked a loose strand of hair behind her ear.

Slowly her eyes connected with his, causing her heartbeat to accelerate. "I just wish you'd come to the pond
that night."

He paused and leaned closer. His breath warmed her
cheek and he took her into his arms. "I do, too, Joy. You
have no idea how bad I wanted to be there."

She could easily get lost in the moment and allow
herself to get carried back to a happier time. But those
happy memories had been buried deep. What she'd discovered after that night ran far deeper than she'd ever
allow Nick to know. As much as she longed to stop time
and stay in his arms forever, she tore herself from his
embrace, leaving his tender touch a distant memory.

"I'm sorry, Joy. I didn't—"

Springing to her feet, she raced to the door, not allowing her twisted ankle to impede her escape. She couldn't
stay with Nick another minute. No matter how much she
wanted to once again feel his lips against hers, their love
story had ended that night at the pond. She had learned
in the worst way possible that, in life, there was no such
thing as a happy ending.

On Sunday evening the agonizing guilt Nick had lugged
around since the previous weekend, when he'd learned
about the assault, felt like a suitcase filled with cement
blocks. It had been magnified on Tuesday during their
rehearsal when he'd realized why she had an aversion to

Little Red Riding Hood. The Big Bad Wolf had been a constant reminder of Scotty. He'd asked Joy if he should speak with Mr. Jacobson about doing another play, but she'd insisted it was too late to start again—just like it was too late for them.

He couldn't stop thinking about what Joy had revealed to him in the shed. His failure to meet her at the pond had put her through the worst possible torture he couldn't begin to imagine. Now he was back trying to steal her dream job. He had to make things right between the two of them. At least this was one mistake in his life there could still be time to fix. He had a plan for both of them to get what they wanted and that was the reason for their dinner tonight. He had to remind himself it wasn't a real date, as that could lead to something more serious. He'd already learned he wasn't marriage material.

"Daddy, what time are Miss Kelliher and Bella coming?" Tyler asked from across the kitchen.

"They should be here any moment, son." When Nick had invited Joy out for dinner, to discuss an idea he had, he wasn't sure if she'd agree. At first she said she couldn't because even though Faith had been discharged from the hospital, Bella was coming over for a girls' night sleepover, but he figured that was only an excuse. He knew the night in the shed had been emotionally draining for her. For a moment, when he'd held her close, he'd felt that familiar connection. When she'd abruptly pulled away, he assumed she had as well. It had taken him by surprise—and created concern. He wasn't good enough for her... She deserved so much better than someone like him.

Moments later when the doorbell sounded, Nick's heart skipped a beat in anticipation of seeing Joy. Tonight would be the first night in years they would spend alone. He had to admit, he had a few butterflies.

The boys took off toward the front door to greet their friend. Nick trailed behind as his pulse raced.

Tyler peeked out of the living room window and his shoulders dropped. "Oh, man, it's only the babysitter."

Nick wasn't sure about Mrs. Whipple's age, but she'd been offering babysitting services since he'd been a young boy.

Jordan opened the door. "Hello, ma'am."

Mrs. Whipple clutched her tiny pocketbook in one hand and a tote bag overflowing with yarn and knitting needles in the other. Her hair was snow-white, as it had always been. "Hello there. You're certainly a polite young man." She stepped inside. "I'm Mrs. Whipple and what is your name?"

"Johdun." He pointed to Tyler, who was climbing on the sofa. "That's Tyluh."

"Oh, my, twins are such fun." She winked at Nick.

"Welcome to our home. Please, come inside." Nick gazed at her full hands. "Can I take either of those for you?"

"Yes, thank you. Your home is so beautiful, but it could use a woman's touch," she said as she scanned the room.

They headed back into the kitchen and Nick stowed her things on the corner desk. "I hope you don't mind, but I've added one more child to the mix tonight, Bella Carlson."

She clapped her wrinkled hands together and smiled. "Oh, wonderful. I love little Bella. She's such a sweet girl."

"Of course, I'll pay you extra for a third child."

She headed to the sink and turned on the faucet. After

squirting a dollop of soap into her hands, she began to scrub. "You'll do no such thing. I love children, so the more the merrier."

This woman was too good to be true. Since the boys lost their mother, they'd never been left with a baby-sitter. What if something were to happen to them while he was gone? The guilt would have been more than he could bear. But after some therapy sessions, he'd finally realized he had to learn to trust an outsider. After all, his wife had died on his watch.

"You'll be well compensated for your time."

Tyler walked over to Mrs. Whipple as she dried her hands on a red-and-white-striped dishcloth. "Do you like to do jigsaw puzzles, ma'am?"

She laughed. "Yes, dear, but please call me Whippy. That's what all of the kids in Whispering Slopes call me."

"Whippy!" both of the boys repeated as they broke out in giggles.

"Why do they call you that?" Jordan asked with an intent stare.

Nick was a little curious himself.

"Well, it's my name, for one, but also because I always put a dollop of whipped cream in my coffee," she said with pride. "It adds the perfect amount of sweetness."

"I like that name." Tyler grinned at the elderly woman.

What a gem. Nick would have to make a point of taking a night off to go out now and then. He couldn't help but wonder if, after tonight, he'd ask Joy to accompany him again.

His heart pounded once again at the sound of the doorbell.

"Bella!" The twins cheered and headed off to greet her.

"They're certainly energetic." Whippy smiled.

"You have no idea. Excuse me, please." Nick walked out of the kitchen and stopped dead in his tracks. Joy stood at the front door, her chestnut hair cascaded over her shoulders in loose waves. The light pink leather coat she wore gave her complexion a warm glow. When he started to speak, his tongue was tangled. *Boy, am I in big trouble.* He needed to get a grip or he'd end up being a blubbering fool tonight.

"Uncle Nick— Oops!" She glanced at her aunt. "I mean Mr. Nick!" Bella ran to him, dressed in a neon yellow coat and blue jeans. She took a flying leap into his arms.

"Hi, Bella. It's good to see you, too," he laughed and placed her back on the ground. "The boys have been looking forward to your visit."

Jordan stepped toward her. "Guess who's babysitting us tonight?"

She scanned the room. "Whippy!" Bella headed across the room and hugged the woman.

Nick turned his attention back to Joy. "Please come in. Can I get you something to drink? Iced tea, water or maybe a soda?"

"Oh, no. Thank you, though. By the way, great job on the babysitter selection. All of the children in town adore her."

Right now, the only woman he adored was the beautiful creature standing in front of him. He couldn't seem to pull his eyes away from her. Or speak.

"Nick?" She rested her hand on his arm. "Are you okay?"

He flinched at her touch. "Yes. I'm sorry. Let's go on

into the kitchen. I need to get Mrs. Whipple—I mean, Whippy—squared away with pizza money."

Thirty-five minutes later, the striking couple caused heads to turn as the hostess guided Nick and Joy to their seats inside of Nick's favorite Italian restaurant. Several generations of the Romano family had run That's Amore. He'd brought Joy here on their first date. Apart from terrific food, the atmosphere couldn't be beat. Flickering candles paired with dim overhead lighting provided a romantic backdrop for the perfect date. But this wasn't a date—was it? Perhaps this wasn't the best place to discuss his plan.

He wasn't sure if it was the sweet smell of her jasmine fragrance or the way the lighting cast a warm glow across Joy's face, but his head started to spin. Reaching for his glass of ice water, he lifted it from the table and guzzled it in one long gulp.

"Thirsty?" She smiled.

"Actually, I'm a bit nervous."

Joy fingered her cloth napkin draped across her lap. "Why? It's just a dinner, remember? You said you had something you wanted to discuss."

He wasn't quite ready to bring up his plan. For now, he was content to drink in her beauty and enjoy this romantic setting. Lately, his imagination seemed to be in overdrive. Being married to Joy and raising the boys together and, who knew, maybe a couple of children of their own. But those thoughts could never become reality without him coming clean about what kind of husband he had been. But people could change, right? Would Joy be able to give him a second chance, once she knew the truth? Doubtful. He didn't trust himself to be a good partner, so why would he expect her to, especially after he'd abandoned her?

"Are you okay?" Joy asked.

"Do you remember the first time we came here?"

A warm smile crossed her lips.

This was good. Maybe she had the same fond memories of this place that he had. Of course, the time spent here was before he left and she lost all trust in men.

She gazed around the room. "Of course I do. You were so nervous."

"What? Are you kidding? I'd scored a date with the most beautiful girl in Whispering Slopes. I was completely confident." That couldn't have been farther from the truth. He remembered his stomach had felt like it was full of a couple dozen bats when he'd rung the doorbell at her grandparents' house.

"Oh, come on, Nick," she laughed. "When you picked me up and walked me to the car, your hands were shaking so bad you would have thought the temperature was minus zero, but it was the middle of summer."

Yep…that sounded about right. He only hoped she didn't remember what happened next.

"And then…"

Oh, great, she did.

As Joy laughed out loud, the elderly couple seated at a nearby table looked over at her and smiled. "You put the key into the ignition and the car wouldn't start. You went into a total panic."

He'd never been so mortified in his life. Now, sitting across from her after they'd both experienced so much during their time apart, he could laugh at himself. "All right, I remember. I'd been so nervous when I got out of the car at your house I'd just yanked the keys from the ignition and forgotten to put the car into Park."

"You were ready to call a tow truck when I spotted the problem." She tucked a strand of hair behind her ear. "All I can say is it was a good thing you were parked on a flat surface."

They both shared a good long laugh until the waiter approached to take their order.

He and Joy had always ordered the same thing: spaghetti and meatballs along with a tomato-and-basil salad and a side order of garlic bread to share. He wondered if she'd remember.

Joy placed her menu on the table and locked eyes with him. "The usual?"

Her vivid memory caused Nick's heart to beat in an accelerated rhythm. With soft Italian music filling the air, he turned to the young man waiting with a pad of paper and a pencil and placed the order—their usual.

By the time the waiter cleared the plates, every morsel had been eaten, with the exception of half a piece of Joy's bread.

"I see you still have that healthy appetite." He smiled, wondering where she put it all.

She leaned back in the chair. "I'll have to go walking tomorrow. My ankle feels back to normal, so I should be able to start running again by next week."

"I might have to join you." He couldn't think of a better way to start his day than a long walk or run with Joy. Having the boys tag along would be nice, too.

The server returned to their table with smaller menus in his hand. "Can I offer both of you dessert?" He handed them each a listing.

Joy released a long breath. "I'm not sure where I'd put it."

They'd always complained about being stuffed after their meal, but they still liked to share a cannoli.

She tossed him a devious smile and nodded.

"One cannoli—two forks," he instructed the young man.

"And two espressos, please," Joy added. "I'm so relaxed. This is nice."

The waiter scribbled on his pad, took the menus and headed off to the kitchen.

Joy clasped her hands together in front of her. "So, what was it you wanted to discuss?"

Unsure of how receptive she'd be, he took a deep breath. "Actually, I wanted to talk about our upcoming interviews."

Joy's back straightened. "Do you really want to spoil the evening by trying to convince me I'm not qualified for the position?"

He reached across the table and covered her hand with his own. "Of course not. The past couple of weeks, I've watched you with the children—you're amazing with them…especially with Jordan and Tyler. You're more than qualified to become principal with or without the master's degree."

"Thank you. I needed to hear that. Lately, a lot of insecurities I thought were under control have resurfaced."

Had his return to Whispering Slopes caused her angst? Or could her rehashing that horrible night be playing a part? He had hoped talking about it and bringing it out into the open would help her with the healing process. Of course, he couldn't even imagine experiencing a violent attack like she had.

He gave her hand a quick squeeze. "Personally, I think you're the strongest woman I've ever known."

The conversation quieted when the waiter brought the coffee and dessert. He placed it on the table and put his hands behind his back. "Let me know if you need anything else." He scurried off to his next table.

Nick passed the fork to Joy. "Here, take a bite. I think a little bit of sugar is just what we need."

She smiled and speared the cannoli.

"Are you sure you can handle that big bite?"

Joy nodded and slid an oversize helping into her mouth. "Mmm…it's just as delicious as I remember."

He laughed. It was nice to see her enjoying herself. Many times since he'd returned to Whispering Slopes he'd noticed so much sadness in her eyes and now he knew why. But at this moment, she was the old Joy who he'd loved so much.

With her fork halfway to her mouth, she stopped. "What's the matter? Don't you want a taste?"

"Of course." He cut a bite and crammed it into his mouth. "I'm not going to let you eat the entire piece alone." Being here with Joy, he'd almost felt that God was offering him another opportunity, but maybe that was wishful thinking. "Yum…it's delicious." He smiled. The treat melted in his mouth, but the bitter taste of his past mistakes still lingered.

With no crumb left behind, Joy sipped on her espresso. "We don't need to discuss the interviews any longer because there will only be one—yours." She rolled her eyes away from his and stared at her coffee cup.

He couldn't believe his ears. Something wasn't adding up. This was her dream. "I don't understand."

"I'm going to cancel my appointment. Faith's doctor

is erring on the side of caution and wants to perform a C-section a week from tomorrow. It's the same time as my interview." Her shoulders notched down and she looked defeated.

"I'm sorry to hear about Faith, but I'm sure, given the circumstances, the board will reschedule."

She looked up at him. "I'm beginning to think this is a sign."

He scratched his temple. This was crazy. She wanted this position more than anything. Why would she give up now? "That's nonsense. This is what you want."

"Honestly, Nick, lately I have no idea what I want." She paused. "Besides, you're a much more desirable candidate than I am."

He'd never heard Joy talk this way. She'd always been a fighter. "I can't agree with that. I don't have over ten years of experience at that school—you do."

Nick reached across the table. Her hand felt like satin under his fingertips. "Promise me you'll reschedule."

Her cell phone chirped, not allowing her a chance to respond. "I'm sorry. I left this on because of Faith."

He missed the feel of her skin when he pulled his hand away. "No, of course."

Fear washed over her face as she took the call. She hung up and sprang from her chair. "It's Faith. Joshua has taken her back to the emergency room. I have to go."

He whipped his wallet from his pocket and threw a wad of bills on the table. The cash took care of their bill and provided a hefty tip for their waiter. "I'll get you to the hospital."

Inside the car, he jammed the key into the ignition and the motor charged to life. "Don't worry, Joy. Your sister is strong. She and the babies will be okay."

As he hugged the dark winding curves of the mountain roads, he prayed he was right about Faith and her children. One thing he knew for sure: this woman sitting next to him was willing to give up her dream for her twin. No way would he allow that to happen. Tomorrow morning he'd set his plan into motion.

Chapter Eleven

Joy's stomach had twisted after she'd received the frantic call from Joshua, and now the snakelike road wasn't helping. She closed her eyes and prayed silently. *Please, Lord, let Faith be okay. I promise I'll work on my jealousy issues. I know it's wrong and I'm ashamed of myself. I love my sister. Please watch over her and the babies. I'm not sure Faith is able to handle another devastating loss in her life. I trust that You'll keep them safe. Amen.*

She jumped at the warm touch against her arm.

"I'm sorry. I didn't mean to startle you. I wanted to make sure you're okay." Nick spoke softly.

She nodded. Afraid she'd burst into tears, she kept her lips firmly pressed together.

They traveled the rest of the way to the hospital in silence.

Her pulse raced when she spotted the red glow of the ER sign. Nick pulled up to the curb in front of the entrance and jammed his brakes. The SUV skidded to an abrupt stop.

Joy unfastened her seat belt and sprang from the vehicle. As she ran inside, she heard Nick saying he'd park and be right in. She sprinted toward the front desk and felt a little relieved when she saw Myra was the nurse on duty.

"Joy! I've been waiting for you." The blonde nurse with spiral curls came around from behind the desk. A good friend for several years, she took Joy into her arms and held her close. "I'm so sorry."

Joy pulled back. "What happened? I thought her blood pressure had stabilized. The doctor said he could give the babies a little more time. He'd scheduled the C-section for a week from tomorrow."

The intercom overhead sounded with a hiss and filled her ears with a loud and annoying static. A garbled voice said something that couldn't be understood.

Myra glanced up. "I thought Henry fixed that thing." She looked at Joy. "I'm sorry. You're right, but this evening her blood pressure skyrocketed, so Joshua brought her in to be checked out. It's higher than it's ever been." She reached for Joy's hand. "I've never seen someone's pressure go that high."

She wasn't sure if it was Myra's cold hand or her words, but a shiver rattled Joy's spine. "Where is she now?"

"The doctor is prepping her for surgery." She led Joy to the waiting area. Thankfully all of the chairs were empty. Joy wasn't in the mood to be around other people, but in that moment, she craved Nick's presence.

"Is Joshua with her?"

"Yes. He won't leave her side. Every woman should be so fortunate to have a husband like him."

Joy knew her brother-in-law adored her sister. Faith was blessed to have a man love her as much as Joshua. Would she ever have a relationship like her sister shared with her husband? Doubtful. Faith deserved it, not her.

The sound of heavy shoes trouncing down the hall pulled her back into the moment.

"How's Faith?"

She turned and spotted Nick. Judging by his flushed chiseled features, he'd run all of the way from the parking lot. His concern warmed her heart.

"She's not good. They're getting her ready for surgery." Joy ran her fingers through her hair as she paced the floor.

"Why don't you have a seat? If you'd like, I can get you both a nice hot cup of coffee," Myra offered in a sweet tone.

The strong yet soft sensation of Nick's hand on Joy's arm guided her to the chairs. He turned to the nurse. "Thank you, Myra. That would be wonderful."

As soon as Joy settled into the cold fake-leather chair, her thoughts drifted to Bella.

"I need to call Mrs. Whipple… I mean Whippy."

Nick slipped into the seat next to her. "It's already taken care of. I've arranged for Whippy to stay overnight, so you don't have to worry."

Was this what it would be like to have a partner in life? Someone who'd take care of your needs without even having to ask? Someone who'd hold a cool washcloth to your forehead when you had the flu? This was what she'd always wanted—the love of a strong and faithful man along with the security of a family. She guessed that was normal for someone whose parents were snatched away at such a young age. Her sister knew what it was like to always feel safe. A twinge of jealousy ran through Joy's heart. Didn't she deserve that, too? Guilt settled in. She should be happy for her sister…not envious. But watching her sister's family grow, Joy had to admit it was becoming more difficult to keep those thoughts away. Was it because of Nick being back in her life?

"Hey, are you okay?" Nick ran his hand across her shoulder.

His touch gave her heart a little leap. A part of her loved the feeling, but she knew those feelings came with risks... ones she wasn't sure she was ready to take. "Yes, I'm fine." Her statement couldn't have been farther from the truth. Her mind was a jumbled mess of wanting Nick next to her, but at the same time needing him to be far away.

"I'm not sure I believe you." He hesitated for a moment before speaking. "I know you're worried about Faith, but there's something more. Isn't there?"

She shook her head in response.

"Come on, Joy. I've known you since we were kids. I think I know when something is bothering you."

She wasn't sure if it was years of keeping her feelings locked deep inside of her heart, or if it was the sweet sound of a voice she'd once loved so deeply. Whatever the case, her emotions swelled like a tsunami. "You know how much I love my sister, don't you?"

"Of course. She's your world. She always has been."

A sense of realization filled her. This man sitting beside her knew her better than anyone in the world, besides Faith. She swallowed the lump in her throat. "Sometimes I'm so jealous of her it's painful to be around her and her family." Her gaze locked with his. "That's horrible, isn't it?"

He ran his hands down the tops of his thighs. "Why do you think you feel this way?"

"Because she has everything I've ever wanted. She has the love and admiration of a man who absolutely adores her." She blew out a breath.

"And?" Nick asked.

This was so hard. What a horrible person for thinking these things, and even worse, now she was confessing them, but she had to let it out. "She has a family and right now it's growing even bigger. It's what I always wanted—the love and security of a big family." Her lip quivered. She didn't want to cry in front of him, but the tears peppered her eyelashes.

When he wrapped his arm around her and pulled her close, the feeling it evoked frightened her. But at the same time, she didn't want it to end. How could this be?

"Joy, please. Don't do this to yourself. You're a good person. You deserve to have everything your heart desires, and you will. One day, you'll have the family you've always dreamed of. I promise you."

Silence filled the waiting room for several minutes.

She wiped her eyes and looked at him—the man who'd once been her entire world and knew everything about her. Now she carried a secret, one she could never reveal to him. "Thank you for calling Whippy." She pushed away the lock of hair that partially covered her eye. "I appreciate it, but if you need to get back to the boys, you don't have to stay." She turned her gaze to the window across the floor.

Nick reached out and cupped her chin, directing her face back toward him. "I know I don't need to…but I want to."

His words touched her heart. "Can I ask you something?"

"Sure."

She didn't want to bring up sad memories for him, but she felt a strong desire to know. "What did you like the best about being married?"

Joy studied his sharp profile as he pondered her question for several moments.

"I don't think I can answer that question. I wasn't a good husband, Joy. There are some things about my marriage I haven't shared with you. I want to, but I'm afraid it will change how you feel about me."

She shook her head. "I can't imagine you being anything but a wonderful partner." In her dreams, he was always the perfect mate. She imagined him to be much like Joshua, loving and attentive.

"Unfortunately, that's not true. My wife, Michelle, was dying right before my eyes and I didn't do anything to help her. Even Jordan noticed, a child, but her own husband didn't. Michelle was supermom. She did it all… took care of me, the twins and the house. She volunteered and tutored students, always going a hundred miles per hour. I assumed that was why she was losing weight. She'd been on medication for her disease and never complained of symptoms. I assumed the drug was working for her." He paused and raked his hand through his hair.

Joy raised an eyebrow. "From what I know about Crohn's disease, its symptoms aren't always easy to hide."

"Exactly. I should have seen the signs. I was a poor excuse for a husband, Joy…a poor excuse for a man."

"I'm sure you did the best you could. You're being too hard on yourself." Her heart ached for him. Nick was a good man, as good as they came. She knew he'd never deliberately ignore his wife's illness.

He shook his head. "I was too wrapped up in my own world, trying to get ahead and make something of my life. I didn't realize until it was too late, I already had everything, Joy. I was the richest man in the world with a loving wife and two beautiful children. I was selfish—plain and simple."

She gently placed her hand on his. "Please, don't do this to yourself, Nick. You can't change what happened. Blaming yourself won't bring her back."

"I only cared about getting my master's degree and advancing within the school system. I wanted the status of being the principal of one of the top schools in Chicago."

Joy watched a tear trail down Nick's cheek. "There's nothing wrong with wanting more in order to provide for your family." Was this why he'd come back to Whispering Slopes to apply for the job? So all of the time he'd spent away from his family wouldn't have been for nothing?

Nick leaned forward and pressed his fingertips to his forehead. "There is when you turn a blind eye to your wife's health. She was emaciated, Joy. I can see that now, but I didn't want to see it then. I could have saved her life… My sons could still have their mother."

Joy shivered when the overhead vent blew a shot of chilly air, but she wondered if it was because of Nick's words. It seemed they both carried shameful secrets from their past that they were unable to escape. She took his hand, and for the next hour, the pair who'd been voted favorite couple in high school sat together in silence. Joy couldn't help but wonder if either of them would ever have the kind of relationship Faith and Joshua shared.

Shortly past midnight with a full moon shimmering overhead, Nick navigated his SUV into his garage. It felt good to be home. Between the birth of Faith's twins and telling Joy his ugly secret about his wife, he was spent. He was somewhat relieved she knew the truth, but he couldn't help but think it would change the way she thought of him.

After the babies were born, Joy had expressed her thanks and sent him home. Part of him wished she'd asked him to stay, but he was touched when she'd told him she wanted to make sure he got some good rest before his interview this afternoon. He'd told her not to worry. If his plan went accordingly, they could both fulfill their dream.

The laundry room door squeaked as he entered the house and strolled down the hallway toward the family room. He smiled when he spied Whippy sound asleep in his leather recliner. Not having the heart to wake her, he removed the afghan from the sofa and gently covered her. She stirred for a moment, but then resumed her soft snoring.

He flung his leather coat onto the piano bench and headed toward the boys' room. As expected, both were snuggled in their beds and hopefully having sweet dreams.

Nick stepped across the hall and poked his head into the guest room. The owl night-light plugged into the receptacle next to the bed cast a light onto Bella's cherubic cheeks.

"Mr. Nick," the tiny voice said as he turned to leave the room.

"Bella, you should be sleeping." He walked to the bed and took a seat on the edge.

"I couldn't sleep. I was worried about Mommy and the babies, too."

The fear in her eyes tugged at his heart. He tucked the sheet up underneath her chin. "You don't have to worry, sweetie. Your mommy is doing just fine. In fact, she's probably sound asleep in her bed at the hospital."

She squirmed under the covers and smiled. "What about the babies?"

"The babies are perfect. You are now the big sister

to a baby brother and sister." How privileged he felt to be the one to share this glorious news.

Her smile lit up the room. "One of each? That's so cool!" She started to climb out of the bed. "Can I go meet them now?"

Nick tucked her under the covers. "Not tonight. You need to get a good night of sleep, first. Your aunt Joy will be by in the morning to take you to the hospital so you can meet them."

She bit her lip. "But what about school?"

"Your new family comes first." His stomach twisted at his words. Yes, family did come first. Why hadn't he realized that sooner?

Bella bounced in the bed. "I'm too excited. I don't think I can fall asleep."

"Well, not if you keep moving like that," he laughed. "Just close your eyes and I guarantee you'll have sweet dreams of your brother and sister." He leaned over and gently kissed her forehead.

As he watched the child slowly drift to sleep, she spoke in a drowsy state. "I love you, Mr. Nick. I hope one day you'll marry my aunt Joy… You'd make a great uncle." Her words swirled in his mind and caused his heart to race. Deep down, he knew this was what he wanted, too. But would Joy want a life with him now that she knew what kind of husband he'd been?

Five hours and a restless night of tossing and turning later, Nick sat on the edge of his bed thinking about the past twelve hours. He knew Bella's comment about her aunt was part of the reason he'd been unable to sleep. When he had dozed off for a little while he had a dream that he and Joy were married. She was sick with the flu and he tended to her every need. He'd brought her soup and fluids, remaining by her side until the fever broke. Of course, it had only been a dream. The reality of the kind of husband he'd been in the past weighed heavy on his heart, and for the first time since Michelle had died, he prayed to God for His forgiveness.

When the weight he'd been carrying on his shoulders eased, he pushed himself off the bed, the aroma of bacon filling his room. He threw on a pair of jeans along with a T-shirt and shuffled into the kitchen to investigate. The meat sizzled in the skillet as Whippy scurried around the room looking as though she'd been up for hours. She'd set a beautiful table and she'd even put some artificial flowers out as a centerpiece. This woman was a dream.

"Good morning." She turned, wearing a flowered dress and a bright smile. "How are Faith and the babies?" She whirled around to give the strips of bacon a quick flip.

He headed straight for the coffee maker. With a packed schedule today, a great deal of caffeine was on the agenda for this morning. "Everyone is healthy." Grabbing an oversize mug, he poured the steaming hot beverage and took a sip. "Boy, you make a great cup of coffee, Whippy." He set the cup onto the granite countertop. "It was late when I got in last night. You looked so peaceful sleeping. I didn't want to wake you."

Her face turned crimson. "I hope I wasn't snoring."

He smiled as he recalled the tiny sounds that escaped through her lips last night. "Oh, no, you were quiet as a church mouse."

She brushed her hand in the air. "I doubt that."

"I'm happy to report, as of last night, there's another set of healthy twins in Whispering Slopes. Faith is doing well and she delivered a boy and a girl, by cesarean section." His heart warmed as he recalled Joshua's excitement last night when he came out to tell them the good news. Nick remembered that feeling and often wondered if it was something he'd ever experience again in his life.

Whippy clapped her hands together. "There's nothing more special than a new life coming into the world… and two…that makes it extra cause for celebration." She headed over to her pocketbook and pulled out a writing pad. "I'll go shopping for new outfits and receiving blankets this afternoon. I can't wait to meet them!"

Nick knew that one day soon she'd be babysitting those twins. "I better go get the kids up. Joy is coming by to take Bella to the hospital, but the boys and I have school."

"Breakfast will be ready by the time everyone is dressed," she said as she took a carton of eggs out of the refrigerator.

An hour later, Nick was showered and shaved and eating the last bite of his pancakes along with two crispy strips of bacon. Obviously his upcoming interview this afternoon had no bearing on his appetite. He was excited to finally get the board's reaction to his idea. "Whippy, this breakfast is delicious." He leaned back in his chair and rested his hands over his stomach.

"These are the best pancakes I've ever had," Tyler said as he speared another piece.

The sound of the doorbell filled the room. "That's Aunt Joy!" Bella announced as she ran toward the door. "We're going to go see my new brother and sister."

Nick stood and walked toward the front door. Joy waited in the foyer, dressed in a pair of black jeans and a wool coat with fur around the collar, looking radiant.

"You certainly don't look like you've been up all night," he said.

She reached for her head. "My hair is a mess this morning."

Nick didn't agree. It was bunched up in a loose bun with a few strands of hair falling around her face, and he thought it looked great.

When she blushed, he knew his stare had overstayed its welcome. "Can I get you a cup of coffee?" He finally spoke.

She fingered her necklace. "That sounds wonderful."

They headed into the kitchen. Bella skipped beside her aunt. "Do I really get to miss school today to meet my brother and sister?" Her grin spread from ear to ear.

"Yes. Today is a special day."

Nick filled a mug and handed it to her. "Did you get any sleep last night?"

She took a sip. "Ah…that's good, thank you. I think I got about an hour or so of rest. I stayed at the hospital until about four thirty this morning." Joy peered around the room. Bella was busy chatting with the twins. "After you left, Faith's blood pressure spiked again," she whispered.

Nick moved in a little closer, catching a whiff of her floral and fruity perfume. He knew she didn't want Bella to worry about her mother. "Is she okay?"

"Yes. It came back down after an hour or so. It looks like she might need to go on medication for a while. The doctor would like to keep her and the babies for a few more days, but he seems to feel she'll be fine." Her fingers strummed the side of her cup. "So, are you ready for your interview?"

His weight shifted from side to side. "I know one thing. I sure am ready to get it over with." He grinned.

"Just so you know, I thought about our conversation

last night. I plan to go ahead with my interview next week."

Following a moment of silence, Nick noticed a look of disappointment flowed from her eyes as they shifted from him back to the floor. "I'm not really sure there's much use, though. After they talk to you, I'm sure they'll know they have the best candidate for the job."

Nick reached his hand out and placed it on her forearm. "Try not to worry so much. Everything is going to work out fine."

"Easy for you to say. You're the one with the fancy degree." She spoke and then bit down on her lip. "I'm sorry. That was rude."

He knew she was stressed about her twin. "There's no need to apologize, but you could make it up to me if you really feel the need." Nick flashed a mischievous grin.

Joy's neck flushed as she tucked a strand of hair behind her ear. "And how can I do that?" A half smile crept across her lips.

Bella's words spoken to him last night had replayed in his head for hours. If he was ever going to stop allowing his past to control him, he needed to take action, and the sooner the better. He took one tiny step closer and whispered into her ear. "Let me take you out tonight… for a real date. No kids—just the two of us."

Her eyes widened. "But Bella—"

He shook his head. "Don't worry about her. We've got the dream babysitter standing right here in my kitchen." He pointed to Whippy, who was busy wiping down the countertop. "Have you ever seen someone set the table so fancy for breakfast? She's the bomb."

Joy laughed out loud, causing everyone in the room to look in her direction. "Sorry." She blushed and turned back to Nick. "Do you think she'd be available to sit again so soon?"

He swung his hand in the air. "Are you kidding? The woman obviously lives for this stuff. Watch. Hey, Whippy?"

She turned as she placed another pancake on Bella's plate. "Yes?"

"Are you available to babysit for this crazy bunch again tonight?" he asked as he noticed the children's faces lighting up like fireworks.

"I'm always available for these kids." She proceeded to clear away the boys' dishes and scurried toward the sink, humming a little tune.

"Yay!" Bella and the twins cheered loud enough for the entire neighborhood to hear.

Nick looked at Joy. "So, what do you say?"

She remained silent for a moment, adjusting her leather belt that hugged her narrow hips. "I'd love to go out on a date with you, Nick."

Her answer made him happier than he'd been in a long time. Earlier, during his prayer time, he'd asked God for another opportunity to prove he could be a loving and supportive partner. Was Joy agreeing to the date God's way of opening the door for a future with her? He hadn't been there for her that night so many years ago or for his wife during her illness, but people could change…if they really wanted to badly enough. Couldn't they? He gazed at Joy, and his heart spoke to him. He was looking at his future. One filled with love, trust and a houseful of kids. He only hoped she felt the same.

Chapter Twelve

Nick's Monday morning class seemed endless. Finally, his lunch hour had arrived and he found himself fidgeting in a leather club chair inside the administrative office of Whispering Slopes K-12. Why was he nervous? Maybe it was because the last time he sat here he'd been waiting to hear his punishment. He and his best friend, Timmy Biddle, thought it would be a good gag to put glue on Suzie Harris's chair while she did her oral book report in front of their third-grade class. Little did they know, their classmate had a severe allergy to glue. Poor Suzie had broken out in a terrible itchy rash that spread all over her legs. The two boys had spent the next week cleaning every eraser in the entire school at the end of the day.

He smiled. Thinking about it now calmed his nerves, as did thoughts of Joy. He'd been thrilled when she agreed to go out with him tonight. If today went well, he'd have some good news to share.

His stomach bunched into a knot. What if she didn't like his plan? If she had any reservations, he'd have to convince her.

For the next ten minutes, Nick reviewed his notes. The chatter of young voices outside in the hall made him wonder if Jordan and Tyler were among the group.

When the conference room door opened, he tucked his notes inside of the black leather portfolio.

"Nick, it's great to see you."

"Hello, Mr. Jacobson. It's good to see you, too."

Nick accepted the elderly gentleman's extended hand. For a guy pushing eighty years old, his grip was strong and his pin-striped suit was immaculate. He'd been the principal long before Nick started school and he'd remained long after Nick graduated. Following the horrific accident that had claimed the lives of Joy's parents, Mr. Jacobson had filled her father's position.

"Please, call me Wilson."

Nick nodded. "Wilson it is." He noticed a brunette woman with a tight bun standing inside the room. Dressed in a thin pencil skirt and a fitted jacket, she reminded him of a mannequin you'd see in a fancy department store in Chicago.

Mr. Jacobson stepped aside and motioned Nick into the room. A long, freshly waxed mahogany table gleamed in the morning sunlight.

"Nick, I'd like for you to meet Mrs. Dixon. She's one of five from our school board. We didn't want to scare you away with a big crowd." Mr. Jacobson chuckled.

Nick released a breath of relief and took a few steps forward. "It's a pleasure to meet you, Mrs. Dixon."

She pursed her lips. "Likewise."

Mr. Jacobson turned to Mrs. Dixon. "Nick grew up in the halls of this school. I have to admit, when I received his résumé, I was quite pleased. Let's all sit down, shall we?" The elderly man closed the door as the three took a seat at the table.

Nick's eyes spotted the icy pitcher of water perched within his reach.

"Can I pour you a glass of water, Nick?" Mrs. Dixon asked with an arched brow as she reached for the container.

His tongue was practically pasted to the roof of his mouth. "Yes, please."

Mr. Jacobson flipped through some papers in front of him. He pulled out one sheet and placed it facedown on the table. "I think you might be interested in knowing that there had been another interviewee besides Miss Kelliher."

Nick's stomach twisted. He'd been afraid of additional candidates.

"The woman had planned on relocating from upstate New York. Apparently her mother is ill, so she had to withdraw her application. So, it looks like it's only you and Joy." Mr. Jacobson half smiled.

Relief settled in. "I see." Nick nodded and took a sip of his water. The bell rang outside in the hall.

Mr. Jacobson cleared his throat. "Your résumé is outstanding, son. Not only do you have the experience teaching in the education system, but you've earned your master's degree as well. I'll admit that is a huge draw for us."

Nick's feet shuffled underneath the table as he thought of Joy, who was working toward her degree. For a second, he wished they were on a more even playing field, but he'd seen her with the children. She was more than qualified for the job.

After forty-five minutes of typical interview questions being fired from Mr. Jacobson and Mrs. Dixon, Nick found himself becoming more nervous. He could sense they were interested in him as a candidate, but would they go for his plan? They had to. He could never take this job from Joy—he knew that now. But at the same time, he had to look after his own career.

Mrs. Dixon eyed Nick. "I think that's all of the questions we have for you today." She nodded to Mr. Jacobson. "Is there anything more you'd care to add?"

Outside the eight-paneled window, a redheaded woodpecker drilled against the giant oak tree. It was the same tree where he and Joy had carved their initials when they were young.

Mr. Jacobson rubbed his hand across his chin. "I know you and Joy have a history that goes way back. I don't want our decision to have any impact on your professional or personal relationship. My only question to you is, if we were to select Joy for the position and you remained as a teacher, would you have a problem answering to her and following whatever direction she chooses to take?"

An uncomfortable feeling crept into his stomach. Would he be able to stay at the teacher level? But he was only a substitute at the school. Would they have him take Joy's position? "No, I would have no problem answering to her or anyone in that position."

He ran his finger down the side of his glass before picking it up and draining the last of the water. Now was his opportunity. "Mr. Jacobson, Mrs. Dixon—" he glanced at them "—I've been doing a lot of research and I've come up with an idea that might be beneficial to this school."

Mr. Jacobson leaned back against his chair and clasped

his hands on the table. His brow arched. "I must say, son, you've piqued my interest." He turned to Mrs. Dixon.

She nodded. "Yes, please go ahead. We're always open to new ideas."

Nick took a deep breath and slowly exhaled. "Have you ever heard of the concept of coprincipals?"

"I can't say that I have," Mr. Jacobson responded and turned to Mrs. Dixon for her thoughts.

"Yes, I have heard a little about it." She paused and placed her pen on the table. "I'd be interested to hear more."

Nick pulled some of his notes from his portfolio. "The idea has been quite successful in schools across the country. It's not a principal and an assistant, but two principals who work together, both of whom have the authority as decision makers."

The two interviewers nodded. "This is interesting. Please go on," Mr. Jacobson said as he scribbled a few notes.

"Well, I believe the philosophy behind it is something everyone could support...two people, one voice. I've read it's quite effective in schools such as this, where it's kindergarten through twelfth grade." He turned to face the current principal. "For one person to have sole responsibility like you've had, I'm sure there were times when the pressure of being the only decision maker was not only difficult, but lonely as well."

The older gentleman nodded. "That's true and part of the reason I've decided to step down." A solemn expression covered his face.

"Exactly, but with two in charge, they're able to bounce ideas off of one another," Nick added. "Of course, there is an adjustment period for the teachers, students and the parents. Some may feel one is more in charge than the other. If they don't get the answer they want from one, they might go to the other. I've learned this is all normal and typically works itself out over time."

Mrs. Dixon rolled her pen between her fingers. "This all sounds positive, but there's one thing I wonder if you've considered."

Nick nodded. "The budget—right?"

"Yes. Two principal salaries aren't within Whispering Slopes' budget. Don't get me wrong—I like the idea, but I'm afraid if I presented it to the rest of the board, it would be shot down for monetary reasons," she said.

Nick had prayed about this issue. He believed in this idea so much that he was willing to make some sacrifices, not only for the good of the school, but for Joy. She deserved to fulfill her dream. After working for the school for so many years, it only seemed right she be offered the job. "I understand the money isn't there. That's why I'm willing to take a cut in salary, if necessary."

Mr. Jacobson and Mrs. Dixon exchanged glances.

The woman squirmed in her chair. "But you'd have a tremendous amount of responsibility, much more than working as a teacher." Her brow arched. "Besides, we couldn't have one principal making more than the other, if it's an equal position. I like the idea, I really do, but it would certainly require some number crunching to work it into the budget, since we'd have to hire another teacher."

Following a half an hour of questions pertaining to his qualifications, the interview concluded. In the end, Nick had planted the idea of coprincipals. Now it was up to Mr. Jacobson, Mrs. Dixon and the rest of the board to decide.

The three stood up from the table and shook hands.

Mrs. Dixon smiled. "Personally, I'm quite excited by your proposal, Nick. Of course, it will have to go in front of the board, but you can trust me. I'll present it in the most positive light."

Mr. Jacobson extended his hand. "I like it… I like it a lot, Nick. No matter what happens, I want to thank you for returning to Whispering Slopes with some ground-breaking ideas."

As Nick headed outside to the playground to get the boys, the sun rays filtered through the clouds, taking away the chill. He released a long and steady breath and his shoulders relaxed. The interview couldn't have gone any better. Both Mr. Jacobson and Mrs. Dixon seemed receptive to his plan, but he knew money would be an issue. His thoughts turned to Joy. What if she didn't want to work that closely with him? Perhaps it would bring back too many memories she'd rather forget. If the board approved his idea, he could only hope she'd be as open to the plan. He pulled out his phone and sent her a text.

Still on for dinner tonight? Just the two of us?

Seconds later, his phone chirped. I can't wait.

Later that evening, the couple studied their menus at the Waterfront Grill. Their table was situated near a window overlooking a lake. A tapered candle flickered in the middle of their table, casting a shimmery glow across Joy's face. Right now he couldn't think of anything he'd rather do than lean across the table and press his lips to hers.

She squirmed in her seat as though she'd read his mind. "It's really beautiful here, Nick."

"I read the surf and turf is outstanding." He picked up his glass of ice water and took a long drink.

She played with a loose strand of her hair and looked up at him. Her eyes sparkled. "That's exactly what I was craving."

He gently closed his menu. "Is that what you'd like?"

She nodded like an excited child.

After the waitress took their orders, the twosome gazed out onto the water.

Nick swallowed the lump in his throat and spoke. "Do you remember the night I told you I wanted to marry you?" He faced her again.

"Of course I do." She released a sigh. "It feels like a lifetime ago, though."

He leaned back in his chair and crossed his arms. "That's exactly what I was thinking. What else do you remember?"

Joy played with the gold charm around her neck, her eyelashes fluttering. "Honest?"

He nodded.

"I went home that night and wrote *Mrs. Joy Capello* on ten pages of my red leather diary." She gazed back to the water. "I don't think I've felt that happy since."

Nick reached across the table for her hand. It was velvety smooth. "I wanted to apologize again for how my father handled our move—for how *I* handled things. I should have tried harder to reach out to you. You have no idea how badly I wanted to talk to you...to hear your sweet voice."

"Do you know what I remember most about your father? How he treated your mother. I knew you would be the same kind of husband." She smiled. "He always referred to her as his 'little bride.' I totally understand you wanting to protect him—that's what family does."

Protect. Sometimes the word made him physically ill. The guilt swooped in again. He'd been fighting so hard to let go of his mistakes, not wanting the events from the past to define who he was and what he thought of himself as a man. "I wasn't there to protect you from Scotty and I definitely wasn't there for my wife." He yanked his hand away and raked his fingers through his hair. "She was wasting away right there in front of me every day and I turned a blind eye to it. Who does that? What kind of man am I?"

The waitress approached and refilled their water glasses. "Your food should be out momentarily." She turned away.

"Nick, look at me." Joy reached for both of his hands. "You've got to forgive yourself… God already has."

"I can't stop thinking about my boys growing up without a mother because of me."

"The blame doesn't all fall on you. Maybe you didn't notice her failing health, but Michelle didn't tell you either. She was the mother of your sons and she owed it to them to talk with you about her health."

Nick stared out across the lake. Lights from massive waterfront homes flickered. He wondered what kind of secrets were behind the walls of those luxury homes.

"Maybe so, but I was the man of the house. I took vows, Joy—to love, honor and cherish…in sickness and in health."

"Can I ask you something?" Joy spoke in a whisper.

The chair creaked when he pushed his shoulders back into the wood and gave a slight nod.

"You said you were busy studying for your master's degree and working crazy hours."

Crazy didn't begin to describe his life back then. The days seemed to blur into the next. But he had a family, so he got up and did it again. That was what a husband and a father was supposed to do.

"Okay, so you were busy and probably extremely exhausted."

He sighed. "It was a challenging season, that's for sure."

"Do you remember during all of the craziness asking your wife if she was okay? Or mentioning that maybe she didn't look well?"

He wasn't sure where she was going with this line of questioning, but he continued to provide the answers. "Of course I did."

"Then how can you blame yourself when she wasn't honest with you? She obviously had her reasons for not sharing with you how sick she really was, but that doesn't mean you ignored her or that it's your fault she died."

After she passed, his world had spun out of control. Dealing with the boys on his own, trying to keep his job and finish his degree, he'd never stopped to think about the events leading up to her death. At the time, all he knew was that his wife had died and he should have prevented it. "I don't know… Maybe."

Joy's eyes swam with tears when she focused on him. "Please, forgive yourself, Nick. It's long forgotten in the eyes of the Lord. You have to move on…for Tyler and Jordan, but more importantly, for yourself."

Silence circled the table until the server arrived with their steak and lobster. "I hope you both brought your appetites." He placed the plates on the table, along with some hot melted butter.

Was what Joy said true? If the Lord had forgiven him, wasn't it time for him to let go of the chains from his past…to move forward, not only for himself, but for his boys? He'd brought her here with hopes of a new beginning for them. It was time to give her some good news. At least he hoped she would think it was good.

Joy clutched her stomach. The predinner conversation had been quite heavy, but nothing compared to the heaviness of the hot, buttered lobster. She picked up the cloth napkin and blotted her lips. "Oh, my, I've never had lobster that rich and scrumptious. It melts in your mouth."

Nick laughed as he speared a chunk of meat with his fork and soaked it in the butter. "I could eat this every night. Couldn't you?"

She blew out a heavy breath. "If I were a wealthy woman, because I'd have to buy a new wardrobe each month. I already feel three times larger than when I sat down."

"Are you kidding? You're perfect. You haven't changed a bit since we were in high school."

Little did he know—maybe on the outside she looked the same, but inside she was anything but the girl he once knew. Years of feeling inadequate took a toll on a person. On a good day, she felt as though there was nothing left of her heart but an empty shell. She forced the negative thoughts from her mind and was ready to change the subject. "So…when are you going to tell me about your interview?"

His eyebrows arched. "I wasn't sure whether you wanted to talk about it or not."

She tucked a loose strand of hair behind her ear and smiled. "I can't deny the reality of the situation, Nick. There's one job and two candidates. You've had your opportunity to sell yourself, and soon I'll have mine."

Nick ran his index finger down the side of his glass. "What would you say if we could both get what we want?"

She inhaled a deep breath and slowly released. "I'm not really sure how that would be possible."

"Well, the interview got a little off track."

Joy crossed her arms and leaned back in the chair. "How so?"

"I presented another option to Mr. Jacobson and Mrs. Dixon. I think they're seriously giving it some consideration."

When the waitress approached, Joy held her tongue.

"Are you two ready for dessert?" She smiled with her hands behind her back.

The uncertainty of where this conversation was headed had caused her stomach to quiver. "Oh, none for me. Thank you, though."

Nick tossed her a huge grin. "Come on—we've got to have a piece of chocolate cake with chocolate coconut frosting."

He remembered. It had always been her favorite treat. Joy smiled, recalling the day Nick had knocked on her front door when she'd turned fifteen. He'd been holding a cake in his hands that he had baked from scratch. He'd been so proud of himself. Even though it was supposed to be three layers, it had been pretty much flat as a pancake. She hadn't had the nerve to ask what had happened to the rest of it.

She gave him a nod. "Okay, but I'll just take a bite or two."

"Yeah, sure. You say that now." He winked, then turned to the young woman. "One big piece and two forks, please."

Anxious to hear about his plan, Joy focused on Nick once again. "Please tell me what happened."

"The idea came to mind after I found out I'd be up against you for the position. I remembered some articles I'd read a few years ago on coprincipals. They'd been quite successful around the country and were becoming more popular."

Joy had heard about that concept, but always assumed it could only be done in big school districts that had fat budgets. "I'm somewhat familiar with it."

"I recently did a ton of research and went to the interview prepared with a lot of positive statistics. Once I presented the idea, they seemed very interested…especially Mrs. Dixon."

Joy's heart softened. Nick had taken the initiative to search for a way that they could both get what they wanted. She reached across the table for his hand. "That was kind of you to use your interview time to try and come up with a solution that would take us out of competition with each other. I really appreciate it."

"Hey, don't be too appreciative… I've got my own ulterior motives." He grinned.

"Really now?"

"Oh, yeah, working side by side with the most beautiful woman in Whispering Slopes… That's a dream job. Who wouldn't sign up for that?"

He seemed so excited. Joy's heart raced listening to his kind words, but she knew the reality. She was familiar with the school's budget. In fact, she hadn't received a raise in the past two years, but that didn't matter. She loved her job, the students and especially the school. "I hate to burst your bubble, but coprincipals aren't in the school's budget. They struggle with teachers' salaries as it is."

The waitress returned to their table with the biggest slab of cake Joy had ever seen.

"Wow! That slice is big enough for the entire restaurant to share," Nick said, passing a fork to her.

He sank his utensil into the gooey frosting and pulled a bite loose. "Here, try this." He extended his arm across the table.

She opened her mouth wide and savored the sweet mocha the moment it touched her tongue. "That's the best cake I've ever tasted."

He reached over and wiped a smear of frosting off her lip. "Are you saying it's even better than my pancake cake?"

When he shot her another wink, her pulse quickened. "Well, maybe it's the second best I've ever had." She took her fork and gouged out another bite.

After the dessert was eaten and their coffee was topped off, Joy turned the conversation back to the school's budget. "I guess I'm confused why Mr. Jacobson and Mrs. Dixon would show interest in your idea when the money isn't there."

He hesitated for a moment. Had they only pretended to like the idea? After all, they'd still need to hire another teacher. No. Why would they pretend? "I told them that I'd be willing to take a pay cut, if necessary, but Mrs. Dixon pointed out that we'd have to receive the same salary."

Joy was speechless, but her heart no longer felt like

an empty shell. At this moment, it was full of love for the man sitting across from her. He was obviously putting her wants and needs before his own. But he had a family to support. She didn't. If anyone should take the lower salary, it should be her. She swallowed the lump lodged in her throat. "Nick, I don't know what to say."

When the server brought their bill, Nick whipped out his credit card to pay the tab.

As they strolled toward the coat check located at the front of the restaurant, Joy didn't want the evening to end. "Would you like to take a little walk around the lake?"

"It's not too cold for you?"

She slipped on her heavy down outerwear. "Not with this, but who cares. I need to burn off some of that cake."

As they stepped outside, he took her hand in his.

Her knees were weak, barely able to hold her up. A cold wind peppered her skin and she shivered.

He hesitated in his tracks and turned. "Are you sure you don't want to head to the car?"

Despite the chill, being so close to Nick again made her feel warm and toasty. Never in her wildest dreams had she imagined they would be together like this again. She felt more alive than she had in years.

Midway through their walk, he stopped and pulled her into his arms. With a crystal clear sky, full of millions of stars, his lips pressed against hers and she melted under the warmth of his mouth. It was real. Her first and only love of her life, Nick Capello, had really come home. But she wasn't the same person as she'd been when he'd left. Kissing would lead to her having to reveal the truth.

When a northerly gust of wind whipped off the lake, Joy abruptly pulled away. "Nick…"

He stepped back, placing a comfortable distance be-tween them. "I'm sorry. I—I thought…" He mauled his face with his hand. "I didn't mean to frighten you."

He was thinking about Scotty. Maybe he thought she couldn't be close to a man. In a way, that was true, but if there was one person who made her feel safe, it was Nick. But she couldn't allow their relationship to blossom into anything more than work friends. Joy knew he'd eventually want more children. Why wouldn't he? Nick was a wonderful father. But that was something she'd never be able to give him since she was damaged goods.

Chapter Thirteen

Thursday evening, the auditorium at Whispering Slopes K-12 buzzed with activity. Backstage, Nick watched as Joy attended to the children. This was their big night. As much as he'd enjoyed the extra time with her that the rehearsals had provided, he was ready for the performance to be over and done. He knew the added stress the play created for Joy. A constant reminder of Scotty was something she certainly didn't need. Like him, she hadn't been able to put the past behind her. He desperately wanted to help her, but he wasn't sure how.

He crossed the stage and placed his hand on her shoulder. "Are you doing okay?" When she practically jumped out of her skin, he knew she wasn't.

"Sure. Why wouldn't I be?" She clutched the clipboard against her chest.

Joy wasn't going to go down that road again with him. "I know it's a stressful time for you. If you'd like to leave, I can handle things."

Her brow crinkled. "Why would I do that? This is our big performance. I need to be here for the children.

Besides, I promised Jordan I'd sit with him while he plays the overture."

Of course she'd decline his suggestion, but he had to offer knowing how difficult this had been for her. She always put the children first. Joy deserved to be principal of this school—she'd earned it. Not only to fulfill her dream of following in her father's footsteps, but after all of the years she had invested her time and love with these kids, the job should be hers. But where would that leave him if the board didn't go for his idea? The guilt settled in a little deeper.

A few moments later, Nick spied Jordan slowly heading toward Joy with a piece of sheet music in his hand and his head down. Nick's stomach twisted as he approached his son. "Are you okay, buddy?"

Jordan looked at his father and then gazed up at his teacher. "I'm nuhvous, Miss Kellihuh."

This was too much pressure. He should have never agreed to Jordan being the center of attention on stage. "You don't have to do this if you're uncomfortable, son."

Joy knelt in front of Jordan and placed her hand in his. "Oh, sweetie, you don't have a thing to be nervous about. You've practiced this piece and you play it so beautifully."

Nick watched his son's brow crinkle as he listened to his teacher and allowed her comforting words to settle in.

"I'll be there with you the entire time. It's just me and you—no one else." Joy kissed the crown of his head.

"Let's do it!"

Nick's heart soared at the confident sound of his son's three little words.

Moments later, silence filled the auditorium as Joy and Jordan took the stage, holding hands.

Chills snaked up Nick's spine as Jordan's tiny fingers tapped the first new notes. Immediately, Nick recognized the song. Michelle's favorite. Of course his son would want to play "Somewhere Over the Rainbow." It was the first song his mother had taught him to play, and now Joy was giving him the courage to pay tribute to his mom.

Nick scanned the crowd, who appeared just as mesmerized as he was by the gentle melody filling the hall. His attention turned back to Joy. She had one hand resting on Jordan's as she watched him, her eyes overflowing with love as she wiped away a tear.

A shiver jolted through his body the moment he realized—God was giving him a second chance at love.

Ten minutes into the performance, Bella stepped onto the stage. Dressed in a red riding cloak, she headed through the forest on her way to visit her grandmother. Nick chuckled when one of the children, dressed as a tree, sneezed. Moments later, it was time for Tyler, the Big Bad Wolf, to make his appearance. Nick kept a close eye on Joy as she twisted a piece of hair around her index finger. Beads of perspiration dotted her forehead.

He couldn't bear to watch her suffer. "Joy, do you want to step outside?"

She could only nod before she scurried out the side door.

He wanted to follow her, but he couldn't abandon the children. What if one of them needed help with their lines? Like a festering wound, the thought of her outside, cold and alone, struggling with the memories of that horrific night, was too painful. He needed to go to her. He hadn't been there for her in the past, but he could help her now.

"Jenny." He stepped beside the young college student who'd been volunteering while she studied for her degree in education.

The petite redhead approached him. "Yes, Mr. Capello?"

"I need to leave for a few minutes. Will you be okay on your own?"

She nodded. "Of course. I know every line of this play. Besides, they're just about ready to wrap it up. Don't worry—I've got everything under control."

"You'll make a great teacher one day, Jenny." Nick bolted toward the same exit where Joy had made her escape only moments earlier.

Outside, the moon was tucked behind a gathering of low-lying clouds. A cold wind grazed his face. She'd left without her coat and his was still backstage, too. He quickly turned to go back inside to get them some outerwear.

With both coats in hand, he trekked around the outside of the school. When he spied her car still in the lot, he figured she couldn't have gone too far.

"Joy? Where are you?" He rounded the corner and spotted her sitting on a bench in the courtyard, by the flagpole where the time capsule had been buried so many years earlier. Her head was down and her face covered by her hands, so he approached with caution. "I brought this for you." He extended his hand to pass her the coat.

She glanced up with tear-soaked eyes. "Thank you, Nick." She balled the wrap on her lap and covered her face again.

"You're going to freeze." He reached for the garment. "Let me help you put this on."

Moving as though her arms were made of lead, she

slipped them inside the sleeves and wiped her tears. "Thank you. This feels good. I didn't realize how cold it had gotten outside."

Nick took a seat beside her and gingerly slid a little closer. "Do you think you're ready to go back inside or do you need a few more minutes? Jenny has everything covered, so don't feel rushed. We can stay out here all night, if need be." Truth be told, he'd like to stay by her side forever.

Joy gazed up toward the sky. The clouds had parted. "It's a full moon, just like that night."

She quivered against his shoulder, obviously venturing back to that dark place. "Don't go there, Joy. I'm here with you now and you're safe. No one will ever hurt you again. I promise."

"I'm not sure I'll ever feel secure again. Scotty stole so much—my innocence and my sense of safety. If only you'd come for me—"

The guilt was suffocating. He should have never agreed to get in the car with his family. Since Joy had told him about the attack, he'd replayed the night over and over in his mind. Each time, a different scenario played out. In one, he'd stood up to his father and demanded he be allowed to go and talk with Joy before the family left Whispering Slopes. In another, his father had decided to wait and leave for Chicago the following morning. In the last vision, he'd caught Scotty in the act of trying to hurt Joy and he pummeled him until the evil boy begged Nick to stop. He had to admit, that was his favorite musing, but sadly, none of those scenarios had happened, and Joy was left with scars he wasn't sure would ever heal.

Obviously sensing his pain from his silence, Joy

clutched his hand inside of hers. Nick turned and looked at the woman who'd captured his heart for the second time in his life.

"I'm sorry. I shouldn't have said that, Nick. It wasn't your fault, what happened that night. I was the foolish young girl whose ego had been bruised. I made a decision that I'll regret for the rest of my life." Her small frame trembled.

Gently, he brushed the loose tendrils of hair away from her face, exposing the porcelain skin that sparkled under the light of a full moon. Emotions from the past and present collided as his heart yearned for another chance. "I wish I'd been there that night."

Her eyes sparkled like the stars overhead. "I know you do, Nick. That means a lot to me." She leaned closer and softly placed her lips onto his.

Nick hesitated, but then he gave in to the moment as though no time had passed. The intensity in the kiss grew as an urgent need to make up for lost time was evident. In the distance a lone coyote cried out for its pack and Joy flinched.

"It's okay. You're safe." He placed his hand against her cheek.

She nuzzled her head into his shoulder. "I feel sorry for him," Joy stated.

"For who?"

She gazed off into the distance. "The coyote… He sounds scared and lonesome."

Nick couldn't help but wonder if Joy felt like that animal. Longing to protect her, he leaned in and grazed his lips against her forehead. "You don't have to be afraid any longer. I promise."

After a few quiet moments, Joy nodded. She was ready to go back inside to the children.

Nick rose to his feet and extended his hand. "Let's go."

As they headed back inside, a barn owl called out from a nearby Fraser fir. Nick could only hope the big bad wolf and all of Joy's fears would be left behind in the cold night air.

As Nick's class enjoyed their half hour of free reading time on Friday morning, his phone chirped, announcing the receipt of a new email. The wooden chair screeched across the floor when he pushed away from his desk. "Jenny, will you keep an eye on things?"

"You got it, Mr. Capello." The girl gave a thumbs-up.

Nick strolled out into the hallway for a little privacy. The screen told him the message was from Mr. Jacobson with a request to come by his office during the lunch period. He could only hope the man had some good news for him and Joy.

An hour later, Nick entered the office of the soon-to-be retired principal. He admired the oversize mahogany desk where Joy's father once sat when he'd presided over the school.

"Please, have a seat, Nick." The elderly man motioned toward one of the two leather chairs situated in front of his desk. "Can I get you anything to drink?"

His stomach was too knotted up to risk putting anything inside. "I think I'm good, but thank you for the offer."

Nick watched as Mr. Jacobson closed the door and strolled across the tile floor. He settled into his chair and riffled through a stack of papers resting in front of him. He cleared his throat and locked eyes with Nick. "I'm afraid I have some bad news, son."

When he'd entered the room, Nick had a good feeling about the outcome of his suggestion for coprincipals, but his bubble was about to burst.

"The school board really liked your idea, Nick. They appreciate your out-of-the-box thinking, but after a great deal of number crunching, they just weren't able to work it into the budget. Our funds have been tight for the past couple of years, but perhaps the topic can be revisited in the future." The man removed his glasses and rubbed his eyes before sliding the eyewear back in place. "I do have a little good news for you, though. Mrs. Murray decided not to return from maternity leave. She said she couldn't imagine leaving her daughter for one minute. I'd like to offer you the position, if things don't go your way moving forward. If you're interested, of course."

The children in Mrs. Murray's class had set up a permanent residency in his heart. Nick couldn't think of a better consolation prize. "Thank you, sir... I'd definitely be interested."

"Great." The man pushed away from his desk and stood. "I better let you get some lunch. Again, I'm sorry the coprincipal idea didn't stick. I really do think it's a fantastic idea and one I hope the board will keep in mind for the future."

Nick stood and his shoulders slumped when he thought of Joy. She'd seemed excited when he shared his plan. Maybe he should have held off telling her until he knew it was a done deal. Had he gotten her hopes up and once again disappointed her? "So what happens now, sir?"

Mr. Jacobson leaned back in his chair and folded his hands together. "Well, since you and Joy are the only candidates, once she has her interview on Monday, the board will make their decision. They are really anxious to get my position filled."

As he headed back to his classroom, he thought about texting Joy to let her know his idea had been shot down, but he'd rather tell her in person. Since he and the boys were leaving for his sister's house, right after school, it would have to wait.

The knot in Nick's stomach squeezed a little tighter. What if his master's degree gave him a little more advantage when it came to the board's decision? Could he live with himself knowing he was working in a job that should belong to Joy? First, abandoning her that dreaded night, and now stealing her dream. If he did accept the position, he'd never have a second chance with Joy and he'd be the same man he'd been in Chicago—putting his wants and needs before the people he loved.

Early Monday morning, with Bella back at home with her new brother and sister, Joy had the time to take extra care in picking out her clothes to wear to work. Once again, she was only responsible for herself. She shook away the sense of loneliness creeping in as it often did in the morning hours and at night. With her interview scheduled this afternoon, during her lunch break, she knew today wouldn't be a typical day of teaching. She hadn't seen Nick or the boys over the weekend, as they'd headed out after school on Friday to visit the boys' aunt, who lived in Maryland.

With Nick and the boys gone for two days, she'd been lonely. Lately she'd found comfort in knowing they were right across the street. Of course, thoughts of the amazing kiss she and Nick had shared on Thursday night hadn't left her mind.

It had all been so unexpected. After running from the auditorium when Tyler had made his appearance, she'd felt embarrassed, but Nick had comforted her in a way no other man ever could. She had felt so safe. She'd given in to the moment and had been unable to resist the urge to kiss him. His lips had been even softer than she'd remembered. But, as much as the thought of a future with him and his adorable boys made her heart soar, she knew the reality of the situation. Once he found out children weren't in her future, he'd move on. So why even start something that would only have another bad ending?

A quick glance in her floor-length mirror reflected a smart black pantsuit with a lavender blouse. She finished off her outfit with black pumps. With her hair pulled back in a loose ponytail, she inhaled a deep breath. "This is it. You've got to sell yourself. Use your experience and the love you have for all of the children in the school and knock their socks off. Stay confident, and whatever you do, don't blow it." Joy strolled out of the bedroom, snatching her purse off the kitchen counter. "Okay, God, I hope You've got my back today."

Fifteen minutes later she pulled her car into the faculty parking lot. Two spots over, she spotted Nick's SUV and her heart fluttered as the picture of him leaning in to kiss her flashed through her mind. She tried to shake away the vision, but it seemed seared in her brain as if by a hot, steamy branding iron. Placing the vehicle into Park, she unbuckled her seat belt. Outside, she rounded to the passenger side, opened the door and grabbed her briefcase.

"Wow!"

The deep familiar voice caused her to jump. She turned to see Nick nearby with a grin as big as Texas and the boys by his side.

"You look nice, Miss Kellihuh." Jordan tugged on her hand.

"She sure does. Why don't you kids run inside and get your breakfast. I'll join you shortly."

The children took off running toward the building and Nick turned his gaze back to Joy. "You look like you're dressed for a big-time business meeting, not a day of teaching at a small mountain community school."

He looked as handsome as he had the other night. Did the man ever have a bad hair day? Everything about him was perfect, even down to his expertly creased khaki pants and shiny auburn-colored Rockports.

Despite the nip in the air, Joy felt her face warm. "I have my interview today with Mr. Jacobson and Mrs. Dixon, remember?" There it was again, that kiss, and now her knees were hardly able to hold her up. *Get a grip, girl.* "Did you have a nice trip?"

"Of course I remember. I was only joking with you." Nick reached for her briefcase. "Here, let me carry that for you." He flashed a warm smile as they headed toward the school. "Yes, we had a great time. Janie, my sister, always spoils the boys rotten. They're crazy about her. I'm trying to convince her to move to Whispering Slopes. She went through a terrible divorce last year. I think a change of scenery would do her some good."

"It's nice to live close to family. I don't know what I'd do without having Faith in town." She paused as he reached to open the door for her. "Do you think Janie will make the move?"

"I sure hope so. I'm going to make sure she keeps the

idea in the forefront of her mind. She works as a travel writer and photographer, so she's able to work from anywhere. She's planning a visit in late spring. I think that's the perfect time of year to lure outsiders to the area. It's certainly my favorite season here in Shenandoah."

Since school didn't start for another forty-five minutes, her classroom was empty when they entered through the door. "I agree. The wildflowers are amazing and so fragrant. It's like living in a flower shop."

Nick chuckled. "I never thought of it that way, but you're right," he said as he placed her briefcase on top of her desk and turned quickly. "There's something I need to talk to you about before you go in for your interview. I should have told you before we left on Friday, but since we left right after school, there was no time."

Joy's stomach twisted. Was he going to say the kiss had been a mistake? She hoped not, but then again, it might be better if they were on the same page. But wait—she wasn't on that page. She was on the page that said that was the greatest kiss she'd ever had. She recalled his reaction, and he'd felt the same... At least she thought he had. Suddenly she couldn't think clearly. Her mind was a jumbled pile of puzzle pieces.

"Joy, are you okay?" Nick stepped a little closer and the smell of his knee-weakening cologne tickled her nose.

Her mind swirled. "Yes. I'm sorry. I guess I got lost in thought about those beautiful flowers." *Good save.* Who was she kidding? She was a nervous Nellie around this man. "What were you saying?"

"Before I left on Friday, I had a meeting with Mr. Jacobson," he said hesitantly.

She knew it. He'd been offered the job. But wait. If

he had been, why wouldn't they have canceled her interview? Oh, right—they had to follow protocol and officially interview every applicant, even if their decision had already been made. "Was it about the job opening?" She was afraid to hear his answer.

Nick tapped his foot into the shiny tile. "Kind of... The board didn't go for my idea of coprincipals." He blew out an extended breath. "Apparently it's not in their budget."

Not really surprised, Joy glanced down at her newly purchased pumps. "Oh, I see." Now it was up to her to wow Mr. Jacobson at her interview this afternoon. But deep down, the fact that she was lacking the advanced degree caused her stomach to burn.

Nick brushed her chin with his thumb and lifted her head. "Don't worry—all hope isn't lost, Joy. There's always the chance they will reconsider the idea when preparing the budget for the next school year."

But that was too long to wait. She had to be principal now—after Mr. Jacobson's retirement. Knowing she'd never have children of her own, she assumed getting this position would satisfy that aching desire. It could fill the void of wanting a family and a husband who would always be there for her. A picture of that man being Nick flashed in her mind. But what if the job didn't take away the emptiness in her heart? What then?

"I don't mean to be rude, but I need to prepare the math lesson for today before the children arrive," she stated.

"Sure. I'm sorry I've held you up." Nick headed for the door, but then turned back to her before exiting. "You'd make a great principal, Joy... Just remember that."

She watched as he disappeared down the hallway. The

chatter of excited children echoed into the room as her eyes glanced at the clock on the wall. Three more hours and the board would be in a position to make their decision. A gnawing sensation filled the pit of her stomach as she tried to remember Nick's last words.

Thursday afternoon, as Joy sat in her classroom grading the spelling tests from earlier in the day, she couldn't stop checking her email. Following her interview on Monday, Mr. Jacobson had told her she'd hear something before the end of the week. Her stomach twisted. What if she didn't get the job? Could she work under Nick's leadership, knowing he'd taken away her only chance of happiness?

Twenty minutes later, she glanced at the clock. It was time to head home. But really, what was the rush? There was no one there waiting for her—no one excited to see her come through the door. As she organized the stack of tests, she heard a gentle knock on her door.

"May I come in, Joy?"

The tone of Mr. Jacobson's voice as he entered her room told her what she had already assumed would happen. The board had picked Nick.

She swallowed hard before answering. "Sure." Her voice trembled.

The residing principal pulled a chair in front of her desk and took a seat. Rubbing his hand over his thighs, he looked up with a grim expression. "I'm sorry to have to tell you this, but the position has been offered to Nick." He paused and gazed out the window. "He was just informed. I know this was your dream, to fill your father's shoes and lead this school, but Nick's degree played a large role in our decision. And believe me, it was a tough one."

As the room spun, Joy gripped the edge of her desk, trying to maintain her composure. She had to remain a professional. She couldn't break down and start crying like a baby in front of Mr. Jacobson. Could she? No, of course not. She'd have to wait until she got home.

"I'm sorry, Joy... Really, I am."

Joy quickly gathered her things as Mr. Jacobson exited her room. She needed to make a quick getaway, taking no chances of running into Nick. She couldn't face him now. In one swoop, he'd come back to town and stolen the only dream she could have potentially turned into a reality. Obviously, her other dream, of having a family, could never happen.

Her heels tapped against the cement as she scurried down the hall.

"Joy—wait!"

The sound of Nick's voice echoing down the hallway only increased her pace. Faster than she ever thought she could walk in pumps, she was out the door, but not before Nick made one last attempt.

"Please stop. I really need to talk to you."

His words replayed in her head over and over as her car hugged the winding mountain roads, and she wondered if she'd be able to remain in the town she loved more than anything.

Later that night, Joy curled up on the sofa with a cup of chamomile tea. For the past hour, her mind had replayed Mr. Jacobson's devastating news like an old rerun on television. Could she really stay in Whispering Slopes and work under the direction of the only man she'd ever loved? Funny, despite knowing she didn't have her advanced degree, she never thought things completely through. Not becoming principal never truly entered her mind since she'd been teaching at that school for so many years.

When the tea turned cold, Joy pushed herself up from the couch and padded to the kitchen. She placed the bone china cup inside the microwave and set the timer for one minute. Her eyes were drawn across the street to Nick's family room window. Bright lights illuminated through the glass, putting a spotlight on Tyler and Jordan. Dressed in their pajamas, the boys were twirling, falling to the ground and getting back up to go all over again. When the oven signaled the tea was warm, Joy couldn't pull herself away from the window. A pang of loneliness caused her heart to ache stronger than ever.

She glanced around the room. Her house felt cold and empty as she thought of Faith in the comforts of her home with a man who adored her and three beautiful children. She tried to force the twinges of jealousy away, but it felt like a heavy weight. Joy loved her sister and she wanted nothing but happiness for her, but it was becoming increasingly difficult to watch her being blessed with everything Joy had ever wanted in her own life. *Stop feeling sorry for yourself. Life is a sum of the choices we make. Your poor decisions from the past have brought you to where you are today.*

Thankfully, the ping of her cell phone chased away the negative thoughts that were taking her down a path of self-pity. She grabbed her cup and headed back to the comforts of her sofa. She reached over and lifted the device from the end table. A quick glance told her it was a text message from Nick. I need to talk with you. The sooner the better was all it said.

Joy dropped the phone on the sofa and curled up into a fetal position. She couldn't talk to him. Not now. Maybe not ever. Once the tears started, they couldn't be contained. Crying herself into a fitful night of sleep, she dreamed of something that would always remain a dream—a family of her own.

Chapter Fourteen

Bright and early on Friday morning, Nick reached for his phone charger on his bedroom dresser. The sunlight filtered through his plantation shutters, taking the chill out of the room. He powered up his phone and his shoulders slumped. Joy hadn't responded to his text message. Perhaps she'd gone to bed early, but he knew that hadn't been the case. Not that he was a stalker or anything, but after texting her, he'd peeked out his front window and seen her lights were still on late into the night. He couldn't fault her for running away from him. Mr. Jacobson had told Nick he'd talk to Joy, so he knew she'd been told the job wasn't hers.

In the light of a new day, he cringed at the thought. Could he really rob her of her dream? More important, could he continue the same pattern of putting his own needs first? Before everyone he loved and cared for? Yes, he did love Joy. He knew that now and every bone in his body told him it was time to man up. He'd chosen his career once over a woman, and sadly, he'd lost her. He inhaled a deep breath and spoke out loud. "I won't be that man again."

The soft sound of tiny slippers scuffing toward him pulled Nick back into the moment. Turning, he spotted Jordan standing in the doorway dressed in his superhero pajamas and nuzzling his face into Maverick's fluffy coat.

"Good morning, son." Nick approached the boy, who still had a pillow crease down the side of his cheek.

"Hi, Daddy," Jordan answered as he placed the dog on the floor. "Mav's hungwy and so am I. Can you make the silver-dollar pancakes for bweakfast?"

Nick reached down and gave his son a hug. "I'm not sure Maverick would enjoy those as much as you. How about I make them for you and Tyler, and Mav can have a nice bowl of his food?"

Jordan giggled as he rubbed the sleep away from his eyes. "I didn't mean for him to have pancakes, too."

Following a quick shower, Nick scurried around the kitchen, grabbing a large mixing bowl from the cherry cabinet. "Tyler, can you grab the eggs from the refrigerator? Be careful with them."

The boy jumped from the table, leaving his coloring book open. "Sure, Daddy. I'm starving."

The clatter of kitchen sounds filled the air. Fifteen minutes later a stack of steaming hot pancakes were piled on everyone's plates. Nick had to admit he'd become a pro at whipping up a quick breakfast when they didn't dine at school. It always made him feel good to cook for his boys.

"These awe yummy, Daddy," Jordan said as he crammed a buttery bite doused in thick maple syrup between his lips. He placed his fork on the plate and put his elbows on the table, resting his palms under his chin. "You know what would make these even bettuh?"

"What's that?" Nick replied, expecting his son to say chocolate or some other kind of sugary treat.

"If Miss Kellihuh was here eating with us. I weally like when she's around."

"Yeah, I do, too, buddy." For a second, picturing Joy seated at the table enjoying breakfast with him and the boys made him smile. He knew what he really wanted and it didn't include him accepting the principal position. Perhaps one day he'd work in that position maybe at another school, or possibly side by side with Joy as coprincipals, but right now, it was Joy's season to shine.

"Come on, kids. Let's get this kitchen cleaned up and head on to school. I have a feeling today is going to be a terrific day," Nick proclaimed as he scooped up the plates. He knew exactly how and where he'd share his plan and profess his feelings to Joy. He could only hope and pray that she'd feel the same.

Forty minutes later, with plenty of time before first bell, Nick had been a man on a mission. First, he'd gone to talk with Mr. Jacobson. He'd told him how much he appreciated the job offer, but he'd had a change of heart. Joy should be the one to sit behind her father's desk. Fortunately, the elder understood and told Nick he admired him for stepping aside in order to make Joy's dream come true. Mr. Jacobson assured him there was still a teaching position available for him.

Nick's steps were light as he headed toward Joy's classroom. He knew that, being the creature of habit she was, she'd have her head buried in the lesson plans for the day.

True to form, when he poked his head around the door, there she was, sitting at her desk and looking more beautiful than ever. Her hair cascaded over her shoulders before she pulled it to one side. He watched as her lips moved slightly with her focus on whatever she was reading.

"Hey." He slowly stepped inside, unsure of whether she'd be receptive to the interruption. She had run away from him yesterday and then ignored his text message.

Joy flinched before pushing herself away from the desk. "Oh, I didn't see you there."

"I'm sorry if I startled you." Nick entered the room and slowly moved toward her. Upon closer examination, he noticed her eyes looked red and slightly swollen. "Are you okay?"

She pushed her shoulders back and brushed her hand across her left eye. "I'm fine."

He could tell she'd been crying, maybe not this morning, but sometime recently. Knowing her so well, Nick knew she had no plans of admitting anything.

"I sent you a text message last night."

"Yes, I know. I was tired. I think I might be coming down with a cold or something." She twisted a piece of hair around her index finger.

Had she fallen asleep with her lights on? He supposed that could be possible, but he doubted it. She hadn't wanted to talk to the man who'd crushed her dream.

"Your text—you said you wanted to talk to me." She straightened the papers covering her desk, looking nervous.

Nick couldn't wait to tell Joy he'd turned down the job, but not here. He knew just the time and place. "Yes, I do, but not right now. Can you meet me in the courtyard, by the flagpole, after school today?"

"What about Jordan's piano lesson? I won't allow our differences to disappoint him. He's expecting me at five o'clock."

Excitement coursed through his body. If everything went as planned, she'd be home to teach his son every night of the week. "You'll have plenty of time."

Hours later and after what had seemed like the longest school day of Nick's career, he paced by the flagpole, waiting for Joy to arrive. After he'd left her room, he'd spoken with Mr. Jacobson again and had gotten the man's okay. The twins were with Whippy, so everything was set to put his plan into motion.

He glanced at his watch, and Nick's heartbeat tripled in speed knowing Joy would be here any minute. The flag overhead flapped when a brisk northerly wind whipped through the yard. After turning down the job, a sense of calmness had finally settled in. He'd accepted the fact that he'd been wrong putting his career first, but he would no longer allow his past mistakes to define him or keep him from proving he could be a good husband, if given the chance.

His breath hitched when he spotted Joy exiting the school. The wind caught her hair as she strolled toward him, flashing a smile. This was a good sign.

"I'm sorry if I kept you waiting. Mr. Jacobson came by my classroom asking how I was doing. He had a silly grin on his face." Her brow arched. "Then he told me the position was mine."

"That's great news, Joy. You deserve the job. The children all love you so much."

She playfully slapped his arm. "Don't try and fool me by acting surprised. He told me you turned down the position. What's going on, Nick?" she asked as she peeked around his shoulder. "And why are you holding that shovel?"

"I'll explain everything later, but first, remember

when you said you wanted to dig up the time capsule? I thought today would be the perfect time to honor ole Mrs. Willis and carry out her wishes." He handed her the shovel. "Would you like to start?"

Joy giggled, sounding exactly the same as she had so many years ago. "Nick, this is crazy. We can't dig up school property, can we?"

"Of course we can. I got Mr. Jacobson's okay." He could barely contain his excitement. "Go on, start digging."

Her smile widened as she plunged the shovel into the partially frozen ground. "This might take a while." She laughed as she glanced at the tiny bit of dirt she'd removed. "I can't remember how deep the hole was. Do you?"

"Not really." Nick reached for the shovel. "May I? We don't want to freeze out here. It might not take me as long."

Within three minutes, the shovel tapped into the metal container the size of a toolbox. "We have contact!" Nick turned to Joy, flashing a wide smile. He placed the tool on the ground and got down on his knees. Carefully, he lifted the box from its home of nineteen years. "Can you believe this? How could so much time have already passed? It seems like a week ago our class was gathered out here entombing a special memento." He brushed away the dirt and stood. "Let's go sit over there." He pointed to the nearby bench perched underneath the massive oak tree.

Their shoulders brushed when Joy settled in next to him. Her eyes sparkled with excitement. "Hurry, open it, Nick."

For a moment, his nerves got the best of him as his

fingers fumbled to release the rusted latch. "It's a little corroded," he said as he applied a bit more pressure. Finally, with a pop, the fastener sprang open.

Joy jumped and clapped her hands together. "I can't wait to see what everyone put inside."

Nick slowly removed the items. Most of the contents were handwritten letters, like the one he'd written. There were a couple of yo-yos, some rubber balls, a few baseball trading cards and other miscellaneous trinkets. When the sunlight hit something that sparkled, Nick recognized it immediately. He slowly pulled out the tarnished gold chain attached to a tiny heart-shaped locket and turned to Joy. "I gave this to you."

She nodded. "Yes, you did—on my eighth birthday." She reached for the piece of jewelry and placed it in the palm of her hand. "It was the most special gift I'd ever received." She studied it closely. "Mrs. Willis had told us to contribute something that held a place in our heart. At the time, this was the only thing I had."

Nick reached for the chain. "May I?" He opened the clasp and extended his arms toward her neck.

She nodded and lifted her hair away.

Securing the jewelry again as he'd done so many years earlier made his heart soar. He remembered at the time the necklace had seemed a little too big on her small neck, but now, years later, it fit perfectly on her delicate frame. He leaned back and admired the chain. "With a little jewelry cleaner, it will be just like new."

Joy touched the locket and smiled. "What you did today…turning down a job that you're more than qualified for, so it could be mine…" She swallowed hard. "You're a selfless man, Nick Capello. I hope you can believe that about yourself."

"I do. You've given me the courage to believe it, Joy. I want you to have everything you've ever dreamed of having."

"But what about your dreams? You worked hard for your master's degree."

He shook his head. "It's not what matters most to me—not anymore."

She cast her gaze at the treasure box that had been unearthed. "Thank you for this, too. When I'd mentioned how much I wanted to dig up the capsule, I didn't know you'd go to all of this trouble…to surprise me and all." Her cheeks flushed.

"I know it's been a stressful time with everything going on, Joy. I have to admit, my motives here are a little selfish," he said, fingering through the box. Spotting the envelope with Joy's name written on the front, he removed it from the container and closed the lid.

"What's that?" Joy's brow arched as she took a closer look.

Nick sucked in a deep breath and exhaled. He passed the item to her. "This is for you."

Her hand quivered as she accepted the once stark white envelope with her name written on the front. Time had faded it to a yellowish tint. "Did you write this?"

"Yes. The night after the picnic down by the Shenandoah River. You'd made peanut butter sandwiches, without the crust." He smiled as he remembered it was heavy on the peanut butter. "It was a good thing you brought extra lemonade." He winked.

"Oh, my, I remember. I thought you were going to choke." Her face reddened. "What can I say? I thought everyone loved the stuff the way I did." She turned her attention back to the item in her hands and gently opened it.

Nick watched as she removed the letter and read the words written from the heart of a twelve-year-old boy. He'd been in love for the first time. When tears filled her eyes, he reached for her free hand. "You okay?"

Joy slid the letter back inside the envelope and pressed it against her heart. "Wait—there's something else inside." She glanced at him as she slowly removed the other item.

"It's a promise ring. I bought it with my paper route money." He smiled.

"This is the second-best gift you've ever given me, Nick." She turned to him and he willed his heart to slow down. "I had no idea you felt that way back then. It's the sweetest letter I've ever read, and the ring… It's beautiful."

He swallowed the lump in his throat. "It's how I felt then." He placed the ring along with the letter back inside the box and took both of her hands, holding them firm inside of his own. "It's how I feel now, Joy. I love you. I know I've made a lot of mistakes, but when I saw you up on the stage next to Jordan, as he played the overture, I realized God has forgiven me. I'm ready to move on with my life—a life that I want to share with you."

The pink hue always present on her cheeks faded when she pulled her hands from his. "You don't want to be with me, Nick." She rubbed her eyes before squeezing them closed.

"What are you talking about? Of course I do."

She shook her head. "I can't give you what you want."

This wasn't exactly the reaction he'd expected. The kiss—had he misread her feelings? Suddenly his heart felt like a tire with a slow leak. But he wouldn't lose her again. He couldn't. They were meant to be together…

He knew that now. He wanted a second chance to protect her and grow old with his first love. This was what he'd prayed for. He was ready to be the husband he had promised God he would be. "What do you mean? Of course you can." He leaned in closer and stroked the back of his hand down her cheek. "You make me and my boys happier than we've been in a long time. They love you, Joy, as much as I do."

Her eyes brimmed with tears as she held his gaze. "You're such a good father, Nick. One day, you'll want more children, and you deserve to have whatever your heart desires." She paused and glanced at the letter. "You wrote in this letter you wanted to grow up and raise a houseful of kids. You were only twelve years old and you knew that's what you wanted."

He nodded in agreement. "Yes, I did—I still do. But I want all of that with you."

His words no sooner left his mouth than he watched Joy as she covered her eyes and sobbed.

Confused, Nick placed the box beside him on the bench. "Joy, please—talk to me. Whatever it is, I can help you." But as he watched her shoulders jerk uncontrollably, he wondered if he really could help her.

Tears streamed down her cheeks as she pushed herself off the bench. She needed to get away from him. If not, she'd be forced to reveal the ugly truth about herself. Her legs were weak as she dropped to the cold and wet ground. "Please, let me go, Nick. Trust me. You don't want to be with me." She wanted him to take his letter and ring and forget she existed.

"I made the mistake of letting you go once in my life. I won't do the same again." He pushed her hair away from her face. "Talk to me. Tell me why we can't be to-gether, Joy. I need to know."

Except for the wind rustling the trees, silence hung between them until she raised her head and looked him straight in the eye. "Because…I can't give you the chil-dren you want and deserve! I want to, I really do, but I can't," she cried out.

There. She'd said it. Now all she had to do was tell him she was only half the woman he believed her to be. That she'd never be able to give him more beautiful chil-dren like the ones Michelle had given him.

"Joy," he said, reaching for her hand, "come back up onto the bench. You need to get off this frozen ground. You're going to get sick."

Her pants were soaked through, so she gave in and rose to her feet. Her legs wobbled as she took a seat on the bench.

Nick ran his hands through his hair. "I'm so sorry. The last thing I wanted to do was upset you. I hoped this afternoon would be fun—a trip down memory lane with the time capsule and all. I had no idea it would reopen those old wounds."

That was the thing. After all these years, her wounds had remained open—they'd never healed. Joy had prayed for healing. She'd asked God for a way to completely let go of the past. Was this the opportunity He was giving her? Would sharing with Nick the unspeakable events that followed the night of the attack release the guilt and shame that had shadowed her for fourteen long years?

When she turned and looked into his eyes she saw nothing but love. Joy knew she could trust Nick. He was the only man she'd ever be able to depend on to keep her safe. Tears pressed against her eyes. She swallowed the huge lump stuck in her throat. "I can't have children, Nick. As much as I'd love to give you a child, it's not possible."

Saying it out loud was like pushing the edge of a jagged knife into the center of her heart. "The night Scotty… A child was conceived." She watched as the sadness crept into Nick's eyes as he took her hand. "A few weeks later, I miscarried. The doctor told me the attack had caused damage and that I wouldn't be able to conceive again." A picture of that day flashed through her mind. Alone, she'd walked home to her grandparents' house, numb. When Faith had asked her what was wrong, she couldn't bring herself to tell her sister the devastating news she'd just received. Somehow, she thought not talking about it would make it go away. She'd been so wrong.

Nick quickly took her into his arms and she was consumed by the warmth of his body. "Oh, Joy, I'm so sorry."

"You're the first person I've ever told," she croaked.

"Faith doesn't know?"

She shook her head. "No. She knows about what Scotty did, but I never told her anything more." It was wrong not to share this with her sister; she knew that now. She'd done more harm than good by not talking about the miscarriage with her twin. They'd always shared everything.

He gently cupped her face with his tender hands. "You were so young. How on earth did you make it through something like that on your own?"

God. He had carried her through events that no teenager, or anyone, should ever experience. If she hadn't clung to Him every day following the attack and then the miscarriage, she knew she would have never survived. "With a lot of prayer and a great deal of denial. I guess

I just tried to block it from my mind. Looking back, I really should have sought out some counseling. If I had, I might not be the mess I am today."

Nick stroked her cheek gently. "You might think you're a mess, but I think you're the strongest and most courageous woman I know, Joy."

"I appreciate your words, but it doesn't change the facts. You deserve someone who can be the mother of your children. That's not me."

"Haven't you ever heard of adoption?" He flashed that crooked smile, the one that had captured her heart when they were young.

For the next ten minutes, the couple sat together in silence. And for the first time in many years, Joy was at peace.

With her eyes closed, she daydreamed about raising a family with Nick. Could adoption be the answer? Would that be enough for Nick? The chatter of little voices brought her out of the dream.

"Miss Kelliher!"

Across the yard stood Jordan and Tyler…and Mrs. Whipple? What were they doing here?

The boys ran toward the bench. "It's four o'clock on the dot, Daddy. Wight on time," Jordan proclaimed.

On time? For what? Joy glanced at the boys, then their father. "What's going on?"

Before she could blink, Nick reached inside the capsule and knelt in front of her.

Joy could have sworn her heart stopped beating, but only for a second, because then a rush of pure happiness and love coursed through her body, finally bringing her back to life. After fourteen years, she could breathe again.

"Joy Kelliher—" Nick extended his hand that held

the promise ring. "I promise to be a loving and faithful husband, if you'll agree to be my wife and a mother to Jordan and Tyler?"

The boys squealed in delight.

"She hasn't said yes yet, boys." He chuckled.

"But she can't say no," Jordan responded, looking as though he might cry.

Joy laughed out loud and extended her hand to sweet little Jordan. "No, I can't. Of course I will marry you guys." She turned to Nick. "And you, too. I love you, Nick Capello. You're the love of my life."

Nick slid the ring onto her pinkie finger. A real ring would soon follow. The twins lunged into her arms as Mrs. Whipple clapped and cheered from across the yard. "Hey, I thought I'm supposed to get the first hug from my fiancée." He faked a pout.

Joy's heart squeezed when Jordan looked up with tears in his eyes. "I knew the day you told me and Tyler we were special, God had handpicked you to be our mommy."

Epilogue

Sixteen months later

"Congratulations, Mr. and Mrs. Capello. You're having twins—girls!"

Resting on the examination table at the ob-gyn wing of Valley Memorial, Joy couldn't believe what the ultrasound had revealed. "Twins? Are you sure, Dr. Peterson?"

"Oh, yes, there's definitely two." The rail-thin man with salt-and-pepper hair flashed a striking smile. Obviously he loved bringing new life into the community of Whispering Slopes.

Joy blinked back emotion. The last year had been a whirlwind, but one she would remember for the rest of her life. First, she'd finally earned her master's degree, and four months after professing their love in the courtyard of the school grounds, she and Nick had been married in a small outdoor ceremony at her favorite overlook on Skyline Drive. The wildflowers had been in full bloom and the Shenandoah sky was the color blue that only God could create in order to ensure the perfect day.

They'd been surrounded by family and close friends. Dressed in a perfect sleeveless sheath gown and carrying a full bouquet of fresh forget-me-nots, she had felt like a princess. The wedding had been a small and intimate ceremony—exactly what Joy had always dreamed of having. She'd never believed it would happen, but Nick, the love of her life, had made her dream a reality. He was her real-life hero.

"Nick, did you hear?" Joy glanced toward her gorgeous husband, who now resembled a raccoon in headlights. "Honey? Are you okay?"

A quick shake of his head broke the trance. "Yeah, I'm good," he stuttered.

"What do you think?" she asked, reaching for his strong hand.

"I think we need a bigger house." He chuckled.

Joy shook her head at her husband, who always tried to make her laugh. "Seriously—that's all you're thinking right now?"

He smiled as he took her hand and squeezed three times… *I-love-you*, their secret message to each other whenever they held hands. "Doctor, could I have a few minutes alone with my beautiful bride?"

"Of course. Take all the time you need."

When the door closed Nick leaned in and brushed a gentle kiss across her lips. "I'm wondering how in the world a guy like me ever deserved a second chance with you." He caressed her cheek. "You've made me the happiest man on the planet, Joy Capello. You've not only blessed me with more children, you've given me another opportunity at life—to be the husband and father God created me to be. He is pretty good, isn't He?"

For a moment, the couple embraced in silence.

Joy cuddled into him. "I can't wait to share the news with Tyler, Jordan and Alexa." Warmth coursed through her body as she thought of her family. Nick's boys, whom she'd fallen in love with the first time she'd laid eyes on them. And precious Alexa, a ten-year-old child raised in the foster care system after being abandoned by her mother when she was two years old. The moment she and Nick had met the soft-spoken little girl, two months into their marriage, they knew she'd been their special present from God. The adoption paperwork would be finalized within the month.

And then two more surprises blessed their marriage. Shortly after Joy had taken over as principal and Nick was happily settled in Mrs. Murray's old classroom, a large anonymous donation had been made to the school. The board voted unanimously to use the funds to have Whispering Slopes K-12 headed by coprincipals. Joy and Nick had been ecstatic.

The second and even bigger surprise was the unexpected pregnancy. When the morning sickness started, Joy thought she had the flu. But after a visit to Dr. Peterson's office, the blessing was revealed to the newlywed couple. The heartbreaking news of permanent damage and the inability to ever conceive again given to that terrified teenager so many years ago had been wrong.

How quickly her life had changed. She'd never imagined the wondrous gifts God had in store for her when He'd brought her first and only love, Nick Capello, back into her arms.

Overwhelmed by the joyous occasion, she couldn't believe that less than two years ago, she'd lived a lonely life in her empty home. Now she and Nick had exactly what he'd promised her the night they opened the time capsule—a houseful of kids and enough love to last them a lifetime. As for the promise ring, it had never left her pinkie finger.

Joy settled up against Nick as they both sat on the examining table, still glowing from the news that their family was continuing to grow. "I guess you'll have to fly without your copilot at school when I go off on maternity leave—you okay with that?"

"If I have you to come home to, you can take all of the time you need, Mrs. Capello."

* * * * *

If you enjoyed A Mother for His Twins,
*look for these other great books
from author Jill Weatherholt, available now:*

Second Chance Romance
A Father for Bella

Find more great reads at
www.LoveInspired.com

Dear Reader,

Thank you for once again paying a visit to Whispering Slopes…my favorite fictional town nestled in the Shenandoah Valley of Virginia. I hope you enjoyed reading the reunion story of Nick and Joy. Two wounded hearts who struggled with the "if only" when it came to their pasts.

If and *only*—two words that can start a person down the road of self-doubt. Questioning things we should have done, or something we shouldn't have done. Choices. We all make them each day of our life. Some take us down the right path while others might send us spiraling into a world of regret.

But what is past is done. We don't get a redo, but we don't have to let our past define who we are today. That was the challenge both Nick and Joy faced, but thankfully they realized God's forgiveness isn't only available to a selected few. It's there for the taking, if we step out in faith and ask.

Remember, nothing surprises God, so let it go! Don't live a life burdened with guilt and regret. He has bigger plans for you, so don't waste another minute.

I love connecting with readers and getting to know you. Please visit my website, jillweatherholt.com, and follow my blog. You can also find me at www.facebook.com/jillweatherholtauthor or email me at authorjillweatherholt@gmail.com. I'd love to chat with you.

Jill

COMING NEXT MONTH FROM
Love Inspired®

Available September 17, 2019

THE AMISH CHRISTMAS MATCHMAKER
Indiana Amish Brides • by Vannetta Chapman

When Annie Kauffmann's father decides to join Levi Lapp in Texas to start a new Amish community, Annie doesn't want to go. Her wedding business is in Indiana, so leaving's out of the question. But if Annie finds Levi a wife, he might just give up this dream of moving...

HER AMISH HOLIDAY SUITOR
Amish Country Courtships • by Carrie Lighte

A pretend courtship with Lucy Knepp's just the cover Nick Burkholder needs to repair the cabin his brother damaged. And agreeing means Lucy can skip holiday festivities to work on embroidery for a Christmas fund-raiser. Will a fake courtship between this quiet Amish woman and the unpredictable bachelor turn real?

HIS UNEXPECTED RETURN
Red Dog Ranch • by Jessica Keller

For five years, Wade Jarrett's family and ex-girlfriend believed he was dead—until he returns to the family ranch. He knew he'd have to make amends...but he never expected he had a daughter. Can Wade convince Cassidy Danvers he's a changed man who deserves the title of daddy and, possibly, husband?

THEIR CHRISTMAS PRAYER
by Myra Johnson

Pastor Shaun O'Grady is ready for his next missionary assignment...until he begins working with Brooke Willoughby on the church's Christmas outreach program. Now Shaun is not quite sure where he belongs: overseas on his mission trip, or right here by Brooke's side.

THE HOLIDAY SECRET
Castle Falls • by Kathryn Springer

In her birth family's hometown, Ellery Marshall plans to keep her identity hidden until she learns more about them. But that's easier said than done when single dad Carter Bristow and his little girl begin to tug at her heart. Could she unite two families by Christmas?

THE TWIN BARGAIN
by Lisa Carter

After her babysitter's injured, Amber Fleming's surprised when the woman's grandson offers to help care for her twins while she attends nursing school...until he proposes a bargain. He'll watch the girls, if she'll use her nursing skills to care for his grandmother. But can they keep the arrangement strictly professional?

LICNM0919

SPECIAL EXCERPT FROM

Love Inspired®

*Could a pretend Christmastime courtship
lead to a forever match?*

Read on for a sneak preview of
Her Amish Holiday Suitor, *part of Carrie Lighte's
Amish Country Courtships miniseries.*

Nick took his seat next to her and picked up the reins, but before moving onward, he said, "I don't understand it, Lucy. Why is my caring about you such an awful thing?" His voice was quivering and Lucy felt a pang of guilt. She knew she was overreacting. Rather, she was reacting to a heartache that had plagued her for years, not one Nick had caused that evening.

"I don't expect you to understand," she said, wiping her rough woolen mitten across her cheeks.

"But I want to. Can't you explain it to me?"

Nick's voice was so forlorn Lucy let her defenses drop. "I've always been treated like this, my entire life. *Lucy's too weak, too fragile, too small, she can't go outside or run around or have any fun because she'll get sick. She'll stop breathing. She'll wind up in the hospital.* My whole life, Nick. And then the one little taste of utter abandon I ever experienced—charging through the dark with a frosty wind whisking against my face, feeling totally invigorated and alive… You want to take that away from me, too."

She was crying so hard her words were barely intelligible, but Nick didn't interrupt or attempt to quiet her. When she finally settled down and could speak normally again, she sniffed and asked, "May I use your handkerchief, please?"

"Sorry, I don't have one," Nick said. "But here, you can use my scarf. I don't mind."

The offer to use Nick's scarf to dry her eyes and blow her nose was so ridiculous and sweet all at once it caused Lucy to chuckle. "*Neh*, that's okay," she said, removing her mittens to dab her eyes with her bare fingers.

"I really am sorry," he repeated.

Lucy was embarrassed. "That's all right. I've stopped blubbering. I don't need a handkerchief after all."

"*Neh*, I mean I'm sorry I treated you in a way that made you feel…the way you feel. I didn't mean to. I was concerned. I care about you and I wouldn't want anything to happen to you. I especially wouldn't want to play a role in hurting you."

Lucy was overwhelmed by his words. No man had ever said anything like that to her before, even in friendship. "It's not your fault," she said. "And I do appreciate that you care. But I'm not as fragile as you think I am."

"Fragile? You? I don't think you're fragile at all, even if you are prone to pneumonia." Nick scoffed. "I think you're one of the most resilient women I've ever known."

Lucy was overwhelmed again. If this kept up, she was going to fall hard for Nick Burkholder. Maybe she already had.

Don't miss
Her Amish Holiday Suitor *by Carrie Lighte,*
available October 2019 wherever
Love Inspired® *books and ebooks are sold.*

www.LoveInspired.com

LIEXP0919

Looking for inspiration in tales
of hope, faith and heartfelt romance?

Check out **Love Inspired**® and
Love Inspired® **Suspense** books!

New books available every month!

CONNECT WITH US AT:

Facebook.com/groups/HarlequinConnection

 Facebook.com/HarlequinBooks

Twitter.com/HarlequinBooks

 Instagram.com/HarlequinBooks

 Pinterest.com/HarlequinBooks

ReaderService.com

LIGENRE2018R2